AUTHOR'S NOTE

Between Two Banks was written in Arabic in 1990. At that time I was ten years into a political prison sentence in Syria, being held without a trial or any hope for freedom. I began writing a book about global economy and politics. Without ever understanding how, this novel started to take over and quickly unfold. I started to wake up in the middle of each night and write until the early dawn, in the dark corner of my cell. In two months it was finished. It remained unrevised, and it was passed on secretly within the prison walls, and read by many people. Since any written word was strictly prohibited, I could not share it openly with anyone in the outside world. People who read it admired it so much they started copying it into hundreds of thin small cigarette rolling paper and smuggling it to the outside via family visits. It outrun me to freedom and waited for me until 1992 when I was released and I published it unchanged, in Arabic in Damascus. In 2016 it was translated to English, and remained unchanged from the original version. I deeply thank all the ones who believed in this book enough to risk their lives and invest the time into copying every word and making these words become alive on this other side, now.

Northern California, April 2016

My dear,

You might be shocked by the truth. You might find it hard to swallow but in the end, you will forget.

I will remain a gentle memory in your life; that is what I expect and want. So please, return to the river of life, drink deeply from it, swim in it for as long as you can.

You wonder why? Truly, it is a difficult question. I myself remained drowning in it for years, collapsing into its embrace, sipping from its waters until I was full. Therefore, my decision was simple; I will leave...!

I have nothing more to give, or to take. I will step aside and let another pass. This is the law of life. It is neither sweet nor bitter. It is a fact and you have to accept it the way it is. You cannot let the humanitarian stupidity disrupt your life.

My dear,

I do not know if I made you happy but I am convinced you were my happiness, my great savior. Even at the end of youth, it was the only moment I felt the will of life.

Thank you for everything and forgive me. Perhaps, I was selfish in my departure but the other side is stronger.

Good bye my friend

Julia

1

"Calm down my friend, it is a great tragedy!" He gripped my forearm in consolation.

"Hah! ..."

My lips felt numb, so I couldn't add anything to my stupid, astonished phrase, as I emerged through the open door.

Pale faces turned, withered lips mumbled softly and then, silence reigned again behind their trembling, shut eyelids.

"Her husband..." An old woman, shrouded in black, gestured to a policeman standing in front of our bedroom.

"I am sorry; you have to wait until the medical examiner is finished." Responded the policeman, shaking his head while waving me away with his hand. His mask of sadness never left his face.

"My wife! ..." I cried, protesting.

"May Allah have mercy on her, there is nothing to do. Rest now and you will not have to wait for very long."

My friend led me to a wide bamboo chair in an isolated corner of the room and indicated for me to sit, saying:

"Rest a little, I will bring you a cup of coffee."

I put my face between my hands, trying to block out this cold black cloud pressing hard against my temples. I don't know why I suddenly had to answer the horde of questions that shrouded my vision. Whenever I tried to disperse some, they gathered with even more strength, crushing my forehead. So, I went back to hiding my face between my hands, pressing my damn temples severely, as if it would release the pressure.

' Enough!' I screamed inwardly, trying to deflect it. Ha, ha, ha ... but in vain, 'you're trying to kill me ... I will go on ... I will go on ...'

*

One day, leaning on the sofa, her face suddenly changed color after gulping down two glasses of whiskey and she said:

"Do you know Selim? I believe life is a will and when we stop willing, we should leave."

"Here we go again with the philosophy! Why do we not just live, period?"

I interrupted her, upset, though I was used to these occasional bouts of depression that attacked her every now and again. Her face would suddenly change color and her crazy laughter would disappear. Then, she would whisper like death caressing mysterious invisible things that hovered in front of her, with nebulous words that seemed to me like enigmas, usually about life. However, today she was talking about departure and for the first time I see her talking about it with honesty. Although, I always felt that the word "life" she spoke of, included its opposite of "death," or rather I could not understand this word except through its opposite.

"Why don't we break up, Selim?"

I regarded her. Silence was stretching a wall between us, her wide eyes covering me with black feathery eyelashes, caressing my face, creeping on my cheeks, piercing and sarcastic.

"Aren't you bored?" Her hurtful voice returned, breaking the dry transparency in the rooms' air. Ivory face with a delicate nose and a rosebud of a mouth, tightened below a black cap of short hair, a mass of little curls.

I worship this small body. I scratch in the corners of my head, drawings for all the swirls and sweet fruits. She reigns as the queen of embryonic things, crawling around in my ribs – green, joyful melodies. So, I adore the wind blowing on my naked body and sink into its depths, the eternal death.

*

"The coffee, Selim."

I let my hands collapse on my knees, liberating my numb head, regarding him with astonishment. His fuzzy voice, like his hair, threatens the frivolous spirit inside me, so it prances towards him in fear.

"What?"

My voice is not mine, deep, floating like the wind.

"Drink the coffee Selim, our tragedy is dire."

I took the coffee cup and sipped a little, trying to wet my dry throat. Eventually, after several trials with his old stubborn lighter that refused to spark, he lit a cigarette for me. Then, he left me alone.

The smoke circles started to swim upwards, then spread into the crowded space of the room. I followed them with wounded, quivering eyes, watching one that kept spinning.

Gradually, it disintegrated into a long comet that soon scattered into a transparent web, hovering briefly over a woman's head, before finally fading into the void.

"She committed suicide!" His anxious words sizzled in my head. I pressed his shoulder inquiringly with my eyes frozen, looking for the sign of a liar but no; he is solid, rigid as the river rocks, showing no features but the tragedy.

"My car is waiting for you. I came to bring you. The police want you."

I remained silent, distraught, not knowing what to say.

"Do not worry my friend, just procedures. Please stay calm. May Allah have mercy for her; she did not want to be a burden for anybody."

A burden! ... Oh, the reckless wind has ridden the land, exterminating the city and heavy stones of civilization. Oh, the wind roars in your depths, flogging your past memories, wild monsters scream in your ears, there is naught but desolation.

Burden! ... The air in the room is a burden, with the smell of death settling amidst it. I am almost suffocating. Nothing is more ridiculous and revolting than this ephemeral woman, pretending to grieve behind her sunglasses, with one hand rubbing her knee, awkwardly.

*

She was one of the first people introduced to me by Julia: her old friend Georgette Nassour. Georgette was middle-aged, blond, with an American face overflowing with greed and a round neck sloping toward her voluptuous, mature body. We had not been long in the city when she visited our small flat. She stopped at the door, regarding me in astonishment; her green eyes enfolding me with such golden feathery eyelashes, that her new black fur coat became invisible beneath their splendor.

"Wonderful." She said, pressing my hand in a handshake. "Mr. Selim, is it not?"

"Yes." I replied, disoriented, trying to avoid her voracious looks.

"Come in Mrs. Georgette, why are you standing by the door like that?"

I stepped aside, allowing Julia to lead her to the big sofa in the front of the room. She removed her coat and gave it to Julia who hurried to hang it, whilst she sat down without once taking her eyes off me.

"Ah, what weather! It has been raining for five days."

"Truly, Beirut is besieged in the winter. Since we arrived we've not been able to go out a lot, though we are wild to get to know this city." Julia stopped for a moment, looking at me reproachfully, then continued:

"Ah, I am sorry, I forgot to introduce Mrs. Georgette to you. I met her yesterday, when I visited their school looking for a job."

"Hello Mrs. Georgette, nice to meet you."

"Thank you Mr. Selim. Actually, Mrs. Julia has surprised me twice, first with her excellent French language and second by introducing me to this young handsome husband."

"Thank you, ma'am." I said quickly, looking for a refuge from her inquiring eyes.

"But how old are you Mr. Selim, you look very young?" She remarked, as if delivering an arrow.

"I am ... I am twenty two." I said looking to Julia for help but she remained silent, smiling, even after I lied and added two years to my age. I didn't quite know why I did that but I sensed an accusation in her questions. So, I found myself answering without thinking, stressing the word "two," as if it were my only refuge.

"Wonderful! Great youth, no doubt that Julia deserves this young man." She said gazing into my eyes, smiling. Then, she turned to Julia, continuing: "You too Mrs. Julia, are exquisitely beautiful. Together, you really make a marvelous couple. How long have you been married?"

I stalled a bit, looking for an answer but Julia was quick to reply:

"We are not married yet. We have an obstacle; we will try to get over it soon."

"Oh! Really! You are lovers looking for safety. What a wonderful scenario! A great love story! You do not need to fear anything my friends, you can depend on me. You are in a strange city and no doubt feel trepidation. Our city is modern and beautiful. You will have freedom and fun in it."

Her eyes burned suddenly and her face glowed with a pink color. She talked with her arms extended, as if she wanted to hug us both. She stopped for a moment, following Julia with her eyes. Then, she lowered her eyes a little and continued in a voice mottled with slight sadness, though her smile did not fade from her wide mouth.

"I lived a great love story too but I am alone now. My husband died recently."

"You are a great human being ma'am, we are happy to be your friends."

"Yes, yes, ma'am, we are happy to be your friends." I reiterated, trying to look into her eyes but I faltered at her voluptuous body; her enormous bosom, most of which was showing from her little black dress, that marble neck sloping quickly to bare shoulders, entranced me. Then, her eyes caught mine, so I escaped again to my feet, watching the light shining on my new black shoes.

"As for you, Mrs. Julia, you will not find any difficulty in getting a job in our school, or another school. I will do my best to see that you get a job soon."

"I am grateful, Madame."

"Do not bother. But I wonder what work will Mr. Selim do?" She said, directing her question at me. I felt her looks boring into me. What do I say? Multiple answers occurred to me, becoming jumbled and incoherent to such an extent that I could not help but say the truth:

"In fact, I have never worked before and I do not know what to do."

"Did you not learn?"

"Yes, high school only. I was about to continue my education in the faculty of engineering."

"Great! But what do you think about working at one of the offices here? It is a pleasant occupation. A friend of mine owns a marine and transit agency. I believe he will welcome you."

"But I don't know anything about such work. It is a completely novel idea for me."

"You will learn. Leave this matter to me."

My eyes were working hard while I talked to her. Bit by bit, I climbed from her small feet, calves and knees to where the end of her dress met her plump thighs. I stopped there for a moment, then made a gigantic jump to her lips, brushing past them to her eyes. Inside me, the panic-stricken monster screamed: 'If only she would leave!' I fled to Julia, to her eyes, to her body. My breast recoiled, reassured. She is still the queen of all demons, ruler of forest nymphs' and night breeze princesses. 'Leave madam!' The voices inside me screamed incessantly, pressing on my chest in demand.

As soon as she left, I clung to Julia, kissing her face, throwing myself between her arms while she pressed my head to her breast and I smelled her warm milky scent. I fell asleep calmly, while she stroked my black hair in grave compassion.

*

Georgette stepped over to me and pressed my shoulder in consolation. I looked at her, forcing a slight smile. She sat on a nearby chair, then she started rubbing my hand gently without releasing my eyes, which faded into her glowing green orbs.

She stayed near me for a moment, then got up suddenly and kissed my face. Her scent faded as she turned to leave, pressing her bag under her armpit.

*   *   *

2

"Abbas has returned to the village." My aunt told her neighbor, while they cleansed lentils on the front porch of our house. I sat on a nearby chair contemplating Salwa, whilst she was absorbed in her book. I had been trying to approach her for a long while but she continued to evade me, without allowing me to draw near. She would smile, or laugh flirtatiously, then move quickly away, pretending sudden fear.

"Damn the girl! Does she think herself Miss Universe?" I muttered to myself bitterly, noting she had not turned the page in a long time. "She can go to hell." I decided right then and continued reading my book.

"Did you know he brought his wife and children with him? They say they came to stay."

"Everyone returns to settle at their home after wandering around. The village is better than the city, 'Om Hazem'."[1] My aunt said, raising her head from time to time to look at her neighbor. "I visited the city last year. I didn't know where to put my feet. The hustle and bustle was like a wedding my dear."

"I saw his wife today. She is very pretty. Though older

than me yet, she looks younger than her daughter."

"Of course my dear! Neither hardship, nor grief. City dwellers do not grow old. Everything is available in their homes. Also, Abbas is rich, as you know. People say they have a servant."

"Of course. I saw her. She is a dark girl. They said she is Egyptian. Abbas brought her last year. He loves his wife a lot. He doesn't want her to exhaust herself in the kitchen."

"Mmm, God bless them!" Said my aunt, with a long sigh as she encompassed the sky with the angry, icy look I was used to seeing when she complained against the grievances of her husband.

"My sister[2], Allah blesses whomever He wants and deprives whomever He wants."

I could not stop myself from listening to their chatter, while trying not to raise my eyes from the pages of the book; I didn't want to allow assumptions to slip into Salwa's head. It was not the first time I'd heard this conversation since Abbas had return to the village with his family and it bored me.

I threw the book down and got up, deciding to find another means for entertainment. One to clear away the leftover tedium cast over my body like a sticky cloak of oil. I crossed the gate, passing Salwa without looking at her, or giving any sign that I care about her. I had decided to ignore her. Maybe this would vex her and she would stop her silly games.

At the village square, I met Saad who accompanied me, telling me how he'd hunted a wild hen that morning.

It was a beautiful day. The sky was free from the recent ghostly black cumulus clouds. It had forsaken its gloom, giving way to some stray, feathery, cirrus clouds. However, the village still bore evidence of the deluge that had persisted for the past few days. Small puddles scattered on both sides of the narrow paved road. Even the paved road was not free of shallow puddles, making crossing it full of the dangers of being tainted with muddy water, especially for those who had decided to visit their friends wearing their new clothes. As for us, we did not fear these mean puddles. We jumped across them to the other banks with the ease of a young Gazelle.

We crossed a side road to the small shrine in the middle of the spacious woods. We sat under a large oak chatting about several issues, not caring about any of them, just to pass time. We moved from one topic to another with the same ease we eat diverse summer fruit. Nothing of a particular taste, everything is equally frivolous when no depth is made of it. As soon as we devour a part of a peach, we throw it away and move to a pear, then a fresh ripe apple that we throw in the river, after merely smearing our teeth with it.

Not long after, the place was packed with hunters returning from their hunting trips. They filled the place with loud stories about their adventures, drifting from one tree to another, from one bush to another, chasing this bird, or that fowl.

Boredom seemed to cling like the smell of the leaf mulch filling my nose. We returned, feeling the bite of a light wind blowing from the west. We stayed silent until we entered the village, where Saad regained his animated vitality. He started fooling around with the girls we met, telling them rowdy jokes. They laughed at him, gesturing their ridiculing of this noisy fool, making me feel embarrassed, so I asked him to stop it. He looked into my face, laughing but switched the path of his humor. He told me lewd jokes, which helped me get over my boredom a little. He stopped suddenly, indicating her with his eyes. She was sitting on her house's balcony, along the road.

"Oh man! Look at those eyes." He whispered, squeezing my arm.

"She is truly breathtaking." I answered, contemplating that woman with her restrained appearance. She was exhaling her cigarette smoke from a small rosy mouth. The upper mounds of her perky breasts were obvious, despite the woolen scarf thrown on her back and twisted over her shoulder, sloping loosely across her breast.

"Look at that head. Does not it remind you of a Greek statue?"

"With some modification." I said jokingly, pushing Saad towards the paved road washed by yesterday's rains.

The long months of spring and summer had elapsed without enabling me to seduce Salwa. She responded to my disregard with more disregard. Thus, I stopped toying with her, deciding to focus on my studies in a better way. I had to succeed in, "Thanaweya Amma"[3] and I had a long academic year. Though I was not passionate about my studies, my motivation was powerful. I wanted to please my elder and only, brother. He was ten years older than me, the driver of a small farm vehicle. He would rise early at dawn, drink his coffee and leave. When he returned, I would have finished my studies in preparation to sleep. He would call me to the room where he, his wife and three children lived.

"Pour us tea, Sabah." He asks his kind wife in a warm, sad voice. She was from our village and he had married her years ago.

I sit near him and Sabah comes bearing the tea, puts it down in front of me smiling and making me feel motherly, tender delight. Though she is not that much older than me, yet I always feel a special sentiment towards her, which flows inside me with warm safety. Maybe, because I considered my brother Ahmed to be like a father to me. My father died shortly after I was born and Ahmed gradually replaced him, without realizing it. Little by little, Ahmed took on the role of a father, then the friendly father.

*

"Do you know Julia," I told her one day, as we were

wandering on the sandy beach in Beirut, "Ahmed is the only one who left a deep wound in my feelings. When I was in prison, I used to spend a lot of time planning our escape together but I would weaken when Ahmed's image rose in my mind. Even when I received your letter, just days before my release, the world still looked dark and dismal to death whenever Ahmed's ghost reared in front of me, his face covered in tears."

"I gave up my children!" She cried quickly and harshly, looking to the sea and wringing her hands. Her facial expressions looked so grim and glum, the black of her eyes deepened, my God! How horrible she looked, like one of those crone witches we used to watch in the cinema, or pictures of witches riding a broomstick. I remember that I never dared mention any of my family's stories after that.

However, my brother Ahmed, remained this constant wound, easily opened at the slightest hurdle I met. I still remember when he invited me to his room at the beginning of the school year.

"Selim, I was never miserly with you. Please, reward me by improving your studies. This is your last year in the village. When you get your certificate, you will go to the university. Please, achieve my dream, do you hear me Selim?!" He pressed my shoulders to stress his point. I answered with a nod, looking towards the silent Sabah, who sat on a nearby chair, pretending to be busy with a piece of wool. I usually took refuge in her when Ahmed's siege became forceful. This day, however, she remained silent, quiet, her face showing no supporting features. Ahmed's mood carried a deep grief. He talked in a soft fluency, his voice warm and low while he looked through the opened window.

"Your father was a man, Selim. I mean a real man. He died in front of me. Rubble fell on him while he was working in the quarries. Do you know them, those large quarries behind the mountain? There, Selim, your father's blood was spilt and scattered on the blue volcanic rocks." He stopped for a moment, looking through the window at the bare shrubs invaded by frightened winter birds, jumping from one branch to another, singing their last farewell. His eyes veered suddenly to Sabah and he started talking, somewhat falteringly.

"He usually took me with him. I would sit near him, watching his hard labors as he hammered rocks with his large mallet, while profuse sweat covered his strong body. He dreamed whilst he worked. He dreamed I would be strong and great. He dreamed that I would be a great architect. I never knew exactly why he wanted me to be an architect but he was keen on teaching me the multiplication tables, until he made me memorize them. He also taught me mathematical problems way beyond my school curriculum, so I excelled over my peers. He was very proud of me, he would take me to public places and announce proudly: 'This is my son Ahmed, ask his teacher about him.' But he left; he left before he could realize his dream. I couldn't finish my studies. I started working before I was fifteen. Life was stronger than me and my father's dreams."

He stopped talking, drowning in the chasm which opened up before him. I did not dare interrupt him. The silence was horrible, full of blood and the tragedy of a person who kept chewing the pain of his past.

"My wish is to realize my father's dream, through you Selim and maybe through my own children, later on. Do you promise me Selim?"

Suddenly, he caught my eyes and held them deeply with his own; while on his mouth, he painted a hopeful smile.

"I promise." I murmured without thinking, taken with this mood Ahmed was living.

I was never certain I would pass the exam, in a way that would qualify me to enter the College of Engineering. However, I returned to my room full of determination to try my utmost best to do so. I can even say that I became enamored with the dream of the College of Engineering. My brother's dreams were transferred to me, captivating me throughout the school year.

The results of the first term were a surprise to everyone. I was elevated from the mediocre students' category, to good students' category. Everyone in the house was happy with my achievements. Ahmed bought me a watch, Sabah invited me to a special dinner, loaded with all the food she knew I liked to eat. Even my aunt, this saintly spinster, did not forget to provide me with her magical spells. Only my mother stayed in her private world.

She stayed in her room as usual, weaving and weaving, as if she were tied to her weaving yarn forever. She would not raise her head from her work, except to answer in cryptic murmurs to whomsoever she imagined was close to her. She would suddenly raise her head, muttering and staring into imperceptible space, wring her hands in amazement, emit fitful, repressed laughter, then return to her task. When I was a child, she still kept some of her memories. Then, slowly, she started looking at me with hostility. She would suddenly push me away while screaming in a brutish manner, which made me fear her. I would tremble at seeing her appearance transformed into a mummy, who wished curses upon her body. However, it remained a fear mixed with love; love inflamed with a confused nostalgia that haunted me throughout her absence in the asylum, where our relatives sent her when her condition worsened.

When my brother brought her back last year, she could not recognize anyone, she remained staring idiotically into space. This made me lose the nostalgia I had retained for long years. Only fear remained, sneaking through me with her intermittent laughs. Especially during those stormy evenings, when her catcalls became mixed with the roar of the storm, spilling through the cracks in the doors and windows.

That day, Ahmed had to vacate one of the two rooms he used with his wife and children, so they all stayed in one room. Despite my great protests, he decisively refused that my room be the victim. However, bit-by-bit, I was able to make his two older children share my room. The room was not big but six years old Samer and four years old Roba, were nice friends. They populated my loneliness with their innocent jokes, hoping around on my back like kittens growling and meowing. Then, fleeing to their beds, when they felt I would start complaining.

They were great friends. I did not have younger siblings, so they were like my own and I felt the elder brother duty towards them. I would play with them; the games I learnt when my aunt was still this inspiring young woman. However, what really pleased Ahmed a lot, was my interest in educating Samer.

However, Sabah always insisted that they leave the room for as long as I was intent at my small wooden table, studying with my books and papers scattered about. She never forgot to bring me tea with her warm smile, which she threw easily in my direction. What a woman! She worked in silence, grieved in silence, laughed in silence. Everything about her made you feel warm and safe; her sincerity, her love, her simplicity, her serene smile, even the constant glow of her cheeks revealed her secret, that secret soaked in loving love and the will of goodness. No doubt my brother was happy with her. I have never seen him angry about something she did, or a mistake she made. Her gentle warm smile was enough to swallow the whole day's fatigue and absorb all anger, or grumbling he felt due to his exhausting work.

In the second term, I persevered in my diligence. My insistence remained great, so I managed to preserve the grade I reached. The pre-exam leave began and the race against time started. I had to increase the pace of my work and wholly dedicate myself to my studies. That is what Ahmed said, when he announced his decision to reinstate Samer and Roba to his room, until the exams were over.

Actually, the exam was not only for me. Everyone in the house acted as if they were the ones who would take it. The house seemed as if it were empty of people, even Samer and Roba stopped playing. I used to hear the admonishment: "He is studying, be quiet." It felt like the whole world had suddenly gone still, announcing a state of emergency. Even the neighbors seemed as if they had declared mourning and silenced their grand radio, which used to play loudly all day with the love songs our young neighbor adored.

One day, Ahmed entered my room with a smile. He stood for a while by the door scanning my face, then asked me with a bit of fun:

"Hello Champion, how are you?"

"Hello Ahmed, I'm doing my best." I said dabbing my face to indicate the effort I am making.

"You will win the battle, as far as I can see."

"I hope so." I murmured modestly. I could not have said anything else. Despite everything, a coincidence, or bad luck could make me fail and that was what terrified me.

"I am sure you will succeed, you worked hard and you will reap what you sowed. Listen Selim; I was visiting 'Abo Saeed'⁴ today. We discussed your studies by chance and I told him about the problems you suffer in studying French. Imagine, Om Saeed volunteered to help you! She speaks the French language expertly and I think she was a French language teacher, before she got married. Also, Abo Saeed welcomed the idea. In fact they are an ideal family; you will enjoy getting to know them. They also want to get to know you and I promised that we will both visit them, today."

I listened to Ahmed in stunned astonishment. Om Saeed, this strange woman with her Greek-like face, is proficient in French! I never imagined she could even read, or write Arabic, quite apart from French. I had encountered her on numerous occasions. Like any other woman, she went about her daily duties, visiting her neighbors, gossiping with them… Nothing significant about her, other than some signs of affluence manifested in her dress and her Aleppo accent.

"I don't know if the situation will allow for that. I have only twenty days left."

"I know that but she will present you with some benefit."

It would be interesting to get to know this strange woman

and why not? At least I would get out of this boring, sad room.

In the evening, Ahmed took me to Abo Saeed's house. He insisted that I take my French language book, so the lady could evaluate my degree of proficiency. It was a big house, its walls built of white, sculpted stones. The hallway was etched with a colorful mosaic. The drawing room was rectangular, divided into two by small arches, raised on round columns. A long corridor connected another five rooms; the walls of which were decorated by small paintings. The drawing room seemed luxurious compared to our small house with its simple furniture. Large sofas, the color of honey, were distributed all over the room along with several small tables scattered between them. Two big carpets covered the floor, giving a feeling of warmth, comfort and luxury.

"He looks a lot like you, Ahmed." Abo Saeed told Ahmed.

"Almost. But he is more handsome despite his swarthiness." Replied my brother, jokingly.

We really looked a lot alike, sharing the same ebony black hair, big dark eyes and narrow nose. I was an inch taller with a bit more muscular build, which gave me more the look of a professional boxer than a school student.

"How are your studies Selim?" asked Om Julia Saeed.

"All right, I try my best but you know how everyone complains about foreign language." I answered her, trying to justify what she will soon find out.

"Do not bother, just make some effort and you will succeed." Responded Abo Saeed, in the tone of the capable authority, stroking his bushy mustache downwards.

His harsh appearance made him look more like a peasant than a merchant. He was tall, a bit lean and dark, with bushy black hair. His harsh features were made grimmer by a deep scar under his left eye.

My brother and Abo Saeed were engaged in chattering about his business. I understood from some words that I could pick out, that they had some joint enterprise. I could have possibly listened better to their conversation, except for my fierce desire to get better acquainted with my new teacher, sitting opposite me. I would take a quick look at her every now and then. After, I would go back to look at my brother, or the walls around me, trying to appear polite. She was sitting right in front of me, a grand lady with her long black dress and woolen shawl falling over her shoulder to cover part of her breast.

"How old are you?"

"Nineteen." I said, trying to avoid her piercing eyes.

"What do you wish to study?"

"Engineering." I answered without hesitation.

"A good specialization." She responded, smiling.

It seemed to me there was a specter of disdain in her smile. I lowered my head as something started buzzing in it.

"Did you bring the book with you?"

"Yes, of course. My brother Ahmed asked me to." I answered in a low voice, still bowing my head.

"Come with me. We can't study here."

My brother and Abo Saeed were still deep in their conversation. Their voices were raised with a bit of excitement, so I thought that an argument might have cropped up.

I followed her to a corner of the room where she invited me to sit near her. She took the book and put it on a small table before her. She started talking in French, looking at my face as if asking me about something. I looked into her eyes seeking help, while the buzzing in my head grew louder.

"Oh, you do not even understand these simple sentences!" She said in Arabic, with a return to her disdainful smile. "Read."

I started reading in a faltering manner. She stopped me with a gesture of her hand, saying with what seemed to me a derisive tone:

"My god, you do not even know how to read. You are very inept!"

I screamed in my head, 'and why else did I come to you,

you …!'

She observed me slowly, in a contemplative attitude, then took the book and started explaining without a pause. Every now and then, she would draw cryptic charts of grammar and other things that seemed to me impossible to understand. Suddenly, she stopped and said:

"Ah, no! This way we will need a long time. How much time do you have?"

"Twenty days."

"All right, I will give you some grammatical exercises that I believe will be better for you than the book. Moreover, we will try doing some exercises from the book. What do you think?"

"As you wish."

"As I wish! What about you, do you not have any wish?"

Her sly smile returned to her creepy, nebulous mouth. My eyes howled in anger and I murmured what I thought was a, 'yes' when I heard her suppressed laughter as she stood, declaring her desire to go out.

"All right, that is enough for today. Come again tomorrow at ten a.m."

I answered with a nod. I felt my head gaining weight, until I could not raise it anymore. I kept my eyes on the faded Persian carpet, while I walked behind her to where my brother and Abo Saeed, sat.

"What an annoying woman!" I told my brother, on our way home.

"What are you saying, Selim? She is a respectable woman."

"As may be but she is so arrogant. She thinks herself better than others."

"No, I think you are wrong. In the following days you will change your opinion."

"There will not be any following days."

"How?"

"I will not pursue studying with her."

"Oh, how ungrateful! What will we tell them Selim?"

"It does not matter. I will manage on my own." I said in a firm tone, making him realize I will not change my opinion. He went silent, trying to suppress his agitation.

The next day there was a knock at our door and a fourteen years old girl came in. I found out she was Om Julia Saeed's eldest daughter, Soha.

"Mum sent me over to tell you that she is waiting for you and you are not to forget to bring your grammar book along."

"Grammar book?"

"Yes, French Grammar."

"Ah, yes." I said astonished, quickly putting on my shoes in confusion. I had not expected any of this, making me forget the decision I took yesterday. It could have ended with that failed lesson. The winds could have blown and carried me over the border into a different world. However, fate was just lurking over my shoulder, dragging me where it wanted. She received me with a sweet smile, patting my shoulder and asking:

"What a lazy student, why were you late?"

"I'm sorry, I was studying and I didn't notice that I'd missed the time."

"Never mind, I was joking. Come in please." She remarked, smiling, while moving ahead of me towards the drawing room, her bare hands hanging down. It was the first time I saw her perfectly proportioned body. She was quite tall, her swanlike silky neck, flowing above the collar of her long black dress. Her small head, oval face, wide eyes and tightly curled short black hair, all hinted at Greek marble statues, full of life and joy.

Everything was normal that day. I stayed until 12 o'clock, then left, thanking her and forgetting my impression of the first day. She was nice that day and I did not feel her smiles to be arrogant, or disdainful like yesterday. Everything went naturally and quietly. The lessons went on becoming increasingly pleasant, which encouraged me to stay more than the allotted time. I even continued to stay until the evening.

In the last two days, I had gotten to know the family fairly well. Soha, her eldest daughter, was almost fourteen. She was a beautiful, smart girl who studied with us in an attempt to benefit a little, at her mother's request. As for Saeed, he was a stubborn noisy boy. He often played in the garden, accompanied by his youngest sister, Salam[5] a five years old, shy little girl. My relationship with the family strengthened, making me feel happy to have found another family. Except for Abo Saeed, whom I rarely encountered. However, when that happened, he would sit observing; intervening every now and then with his pedagogical, meaningless advice, causing me pointless distress.

I can say that I made little progress in the French language, in spite of the few extra lessons. However, the result was reasonable, compared to former results. In any case, my other results were good and I managed to achieve the level that qualified me to enter the Faculty of Mechanical or Electrical Engineering. That was OK as long as it was the Faculty of Engineering. Although, my brother's dream was the Faculty of Civil Engineering but he was happy and he rushed to congratulate me. I was in a good mood that day.

I went by Abo Saeed's house. Om Saeed was standing on the balcony, accompanied by her youngest daughter. She welcomed me while I was still a few steps away from their home. Her face was brimming with joy and she made a victory sign.

"Congratulations, Selim! Congratulations!" She shouted with a childish joyful voice, her emotions peppering her salutation.

"Thank you Om Saeed, thank you! A part of this is due to you." I cried with joy, her cheerful excitement transferred to me.

She invited me inside, hurrying to the entrance to receive me. She opened the door, still sending a magic smile. She grabbed my forearm and gently led me in, saying:

"Come in Selim, we will celebrate your success today."

"Ah, you embarrass me Om Saeed."

Everything was really magic on this day. Even Om Saeed had turned into a young girl with wonderful features. In her eyes, laughter sparkled like a fated storm, suddenly blowing to disperse leaves of oblivious joy in your eyes and face.

"Are not you happy, Selim? We are all happy for your success."

"I am very happy, especially when I find this joy meeting me on this day. I never imagined that I would one day be a friend of such a kind family. This is more than I could have hoped for."

"We are all proud of you, Selim. See, even Salam waited for you with joy. We have come to feel that you are one of us. I made you some dessert, to celebrate your success. Come on, go in and wait for me, I will come shortly."

I sat in the usual corner waiting until she returned, carrying a cake and a small book, presented as a gift for my success. After eating the cake, the young Egyptian maid brought two cups of coffee.

"Won't you smoke?"

She offered me a foreign pack of cigarettes, carrying the lighter with the other hand.

"Thank you." I said in confusion, expressing my gratitude. I was not yet used to smoking in her presence.[6]

"Ah, a cigarette is quite alright on such an occasion as this."

I took the cigarette out of the pack hesitantly, so she hurried to light it, smiling encouragement. Then, brought the book and sat down next to me, showing me how to read it. She leafed through its pages, indicating some difficult words and explaining them. When I felt that she was done, I stepped forward to take the book in preparation for leaving but her hand held mine, not letting go, while she went on exploring the content of the cover with her eyes. I felt the warmth of this delicate little hand, this delicious current piercing my breast and then flow quietly to my back. I looked at her face; she was still absorbed by the book. Her eyes glittered with an enchanting sparkle and her small mouth mumbled, mutely. I twisted out my fingers and pressed her hand softly.

I felt the blood pulsating in her hand and her lower lip trembled as she looked at my face, in bewilderment. She stayed in this position momentarily; then her lips smiled delicately while she pulled her hand away softly, as if offering an apology.

I lowered my eyes, saying:

"Then I can leave." I murmured, standing up in preparation for leaving without taking the book. She in turn, stood, giving me the book saying:

"Take the book with you, do not forget it and if you want I can loan you many others. I hope you will always visit us, Selim."

"Sure, sure, Om Saeed. I feel happy in your company."

She accompanied me to the outer door, repeating congratulations for my success. I walked back to the house, still immersed in those magical moments, astonished by those fast palpitations that reverberated in my chest, as I buried her small hand in my large ones. I searched her words, looking for the remains of a dream to wrap my fancy. "I can loan you many others," "I hope you will always visit us, Selim." ... Is it an invitation? I went back to the past few days, to the slightest whisper or signal, to her blinking eyes as she explained a lesson to me. 'But no! She was always demure, maybe sometimes even cool. Besides, she is married and mother of three children. My God, how could I think like this?! Oh, I must be crazy!' I decided I wouldn't return to such thoughts again. I have to be more respectful of this great lady. Besides, my relationship with Salwa had begun to improve. She had ceased her flirtatious teasing and started to be nice, trying to earn my friendship. Maybe I was lucky; she was the most beautiful girl in the village with her green eyes and long blond hair, as well as her voluptuous, fully developed body. How that body had seduced me and pushed me into a spiral of lecherous fantasies.

I sat in my room, trying to read the French story that she gave me but did not manage much progress. However, the memory of that meeting returned, rushing strongly into my mind, permeating its dark corners and illuminating all the other meetings that I shared with her. Her face looked more mature, her eyes, her lips, the marble-like neck, the body twisted like a python. 'Why not?' Cried out an unknown snake inside me.

The next day I was knocking on her door, citing my need to have some words explained.

"Really!" She said, putting her hand on my shoulder, gently.

"Yes, of course." I answered confusedly, feeling those penetrating looks piercing every cell in my brain.

"Well, please come in."

I followed her, lowering my eyes; eddies of cowardice starting to hover in front of me. Everything in her gaze requested me to back down; yet I decided to follow through with my role, normally. I sat in the usual place, putting the book in front of me. On my face, I put that sober mask, the one I usually resorted to when I felt naked in front of those I feared.

I left a clear distance between our bodies, opening the book to show her a few sentences and words that I found incomprehensible. She looked at me with this mysterious, quiet smile. Years later, this smile would still freeze me in my place, making me feel naked, with those dark corners in me seeping into my face and glowing in large letters.

"Do you have a girlfriend?" She asked suddenly, without taking her eyes off my face.

"No ... Yes, I mean something like that."

She released a light laugh, while closing the book.

"Well, well, no doubt you are shy, or else you would not sweat so!"

"I'm not behaving weirdly, I'm telling the truth."

"And what truth?"

"She is half a girlfriend, or rather she is nothing to me."

"You love her?"

"I don't think so, perhaps I like her."

"Why did you come today?"

"Today! ... I came because of the book. There are some difficult words I did not understand and I thought you might do me a favor."

"And what favor are you looking for?"

"Explaining difficult words."

"Really! ..." She said in a skeptical tone, returning to her mysterious smile.

"Of course! What else do you think?"

"I think there is something else."

"You are going too far, Om Saeed."

"And your lustful eyes pursuing me?"

"I!"

"Yes and yesterday when you pressed my hands with this well-known sign?"

"I do not remember this, it may have occurred by chance."

"Perhaps you forgot your many attempts to cling to me?"

"This was never done intentionally, it happened by chance."

"Don't you have anything other than chance?"

"A lot of things happen by chance."

"You lie, Selim!" She raised her voice suddenly and puckered her forehead.

"No! I am telling the truth."

"Did you ever love anyone in your life?" She yelled at me, her face was red with emotion.

"Of course!" I answered sharply, struck by some kind of madness.

"Who?"

"You! ..."

The universe crashed suddenly, plunging into a deep silence, only the walls started twisting making this hesitant squeak, which clung to my ears. I don't know how this happened! Her jumpy eyes, like those of a cat, her raised voice, our reciprocal yelling. All made me lose my mind, or perhaps my cowardice, so defiant, hot blood surged inside me.

"Yes you!" I cried, confronting this face that had resumed its clarity, defying this light smile heavily loaded with meaning.

"You love me! Ha, ha, ha .." She laughed, wringing her hands.

"Does this happen to you with every teacher?"

"No, I am not a child. Besides, you are the one who encouraged me to do so."

"How?"

"I don't know! All your deeds were suggesting it."

"Liar! You hated me at the beginning."

"Yes, this happened at the beginning. But why did you invite me yesterday?"

"In order to congratulate you on your success."

"And your hand that caught my hand?"

"Normally."

The air separating us was ignited with outrage and challenge.

"Well, so now you know why I came today?"

"You have to pay attention to yourself, I am married."

"So?"

"You can leave."

"And yet, I repeat it to you, you are the one I love."

"No, you love my body."

"What is the difference?"

"Things you would not understand."

"I told you I'm not a kid!"

"I didn't say you are."

"But you do, your eyes betray you."

"Don't be stupid."

"I'm not stupid, I love you and that is all there is to it. The world may go to hell as far as I'm concerned."

"Do not raise your voice; do not forget that I am married. I wish that you would regain your sanity and realize what you are doing. You can rest assured that I won't tell anyone about this. But if you continue in this, I will have to ..."

She stopped suddenly, raising her hand in a threat, then quietly returned it to her knee. Her expression began to wear this sad sympathy.

"Please, Selim, I don't want to hurt you. You are still young and will soon join your university. The city will be yours, with all its joy and eccentricity. You will lose your wonder soon and find happiness with a beautiful girl."

I was listening while observing her face. It was shinning again; her damp eyes glistened with a strange sadness.

Reality began flowing like a grand waterfall, in my temples and down my skull. I lowered my head, trying to capture what was happening. Cowardice returned to infiltrate my blood and that loud insolence which had arrested my tongue for a few minutes, fled. She looked to be in deep thought, holding her face in her palms and looking into the deep space behind the glass window.

"Forgive me." I said in a low voice with my head still bowed. "I don't know how this happened. In fact, I didn't mean what I said."

She remained silent, without the least gesture to suggest that she'd heard what I'd said. However, I couldn't resist this mode, which pushed me to speak.

"I repeat my apologies; I didn't mean to offend. Please, try to understand that. I don't know what to say, I don't know what possessed me to say these things, perhaps anger. I'm sometimes reckless, which is why I always fall into trouble. I promise you I won't repeat this, ever again. I will get out of here and I won't let you see my face anymore. I will be leaving the village in a month, as you know."

I stopped talking and I looked at her imploringly, wishing she would say a reassuring word; to let me leave, acquitted of the disease that afflicted me. However, she remained silent, staring into the void without seeming to hear what I said. Then suddenly, she turned around, moving her open hand forward and saying:

"Do you really love me?" Her voice came out hollow and deep, as if emerging from a well.

"Please, I told you it was a moment of time that I will not return to."

"Answer me honestly."

"Om Saeed, I am sorry for what happened."

"I'm waiting for your answer."

"Oh .. I don't know what to say. But I feel like you are close to a great extent, this just happened today. I felt that I need you. Please don't get me wrong. I can't express precisely what I feel - perhaps I can say: I .. I .. Excuse me, I have to go out ... "

I really needed air. I needed to escape, to hide behind a pile of stones, or a thick bush. Death was swallowing the world and the roar of frightened things deafened my ears. Piles of humanity fell back into the fleeing depths, silence was a trembling neigh pervading the courtyard, empty but for her spirit hovering around my body like a forgotten cloak on the banks of a small stream.

The darkness was not intense, nor was there a bitter cold bombarding the narrow alleys but his teeth were chattering like two angry magpies as he wandered those village paths, covered in their light grey apparel. His colored, infatuated eyes swept to and fro, searching for the remnants of a shadow on a balcony, the curves of which looked twisted from afar.

"Until when?" His trembling lips muttered, while he pitched a bloody branch between his hands. He could have knocked on her door, on one pretext or another. He could have hid under the safe darkness of night, then, climbed a nearby roof to steal those lost looks. He could have thrown those sweet shy words at her as she left her home in the morning. However, he remained suspended behind the doors of the crime. Simply hoping for a lukewarm smile to dangle from her lips, when they passed by each other. He knew that a cynical mystery was perched between her eyes, a bloody war raging in their hearts. 'I worship this mad fear frozen in your eyes; I adore this sleepy melody in your eyes.' The voice of madness cried in his chest, while he slept with his hands attached to a rock wall.

He did not return to visit her, just as he promised. He returned home that day, stunned by a fever of disappointment. He wandered through his past life searching for a haven, a safe spirit to shelter him. Names of dozens of friends, with whom he was dissolute in blatant frivolity, fluctuated in his memory. Yet, none of them could replace her spirit, nor be a haven for his soul.

Did he love her? Something, with unknown features, was sleeping in the corners of his chest. Did he adore her? The answer seemed as distant and unapproachable as she was. All the labels remained cloudy, treacherous, not worth describing the feelings he carried in his heart. Everything burst suddenly and then, fell like a bird shot dead by a skilled hunter.

For some moments, he did not know the secret of her eyes, hidden behind impossible passion. For some moments, passion was a divine secret, unseen by his eyes, filled with the desire to die above the ships mast. For some moments, he mumbled in his permanent slumber behind piles of tranquility:

"Oh God .. Master of the orphaned heart!"

He wandered the village paths searching for air, for a soft breast to lay his head upon and his feet led him to her home: 'Oh God, where are you, my saintly aunt? O goddess of the forest, wet air lady?'

He knocked on her old wooden door, while still afloat in Julia's image, swimming in front of his eyes like fragrant smoke.

"Come in my dear."

He did not wonder how she knew him, despite the closed door. It had gone, the astonishment that used to sneak down his back in cold shivers when she was hit by a hidden bolt, turning her into a saint, swimming in the space of the unknown; reading the thoughts of those before her as you read bulletin boards and seeing, despite thick veils, better than he does in broad daylight.

He pushed the door with his hand and entered into those sweet, comfortable shadows, which flowed from a small lamp hung behind her.

She was sitting on a small sofa, behind a small table, on which a small wax statue was placed.

"Aunt! .. I come to you sad and damaged. I don't have anyone else to turn to."

"Oh my dear, you are tarnished. You were hit by life's arrow!"

"Yes, aunt I have lost everything this evening."

" Approach my poor dear, approach. Let me touch your head."

He shuffled towards her and then threw himself on her breast, his eyes dropped into a deep void. He started to feel this instinctive warmth flowing in his blood, bringing serenity and tranquility. Her hand caressed his hair quietly, as she cradled him while still caressing the wax statue.

"Tell me darling, what do you love about her?"

"Ahh ... I don't know .. Maybe her eyes, maybe her lips or perhaps that golden warm smile. Maybe .. maybe. I don't know what to say. Something in her spirit compels me to death."

"I want to hear everything. Tell me how this happened." She said gently, lifting his head off her breasts. She sat facing him, squarely. Her black eyes sailed in his eyes, away toward their depths. Her black veil fell from her hair, revealing a white profuse waterfall of abundant locks. He began to tell her, contemplating her hair and features. In his eyes he saw the distant past, with its treachery and mercy.

A few years ago, her densely black hair hadn't been invaded by these abundant gray strands, which now fell around her beautiful white neck. He'd always believed that his charming Venus of an aunt, who was endowed with the most beautiful eyes in their village, could never get old. In her body, standing strong and erect like a mountain defied storms, dwelt Eve's permanent charm. She moved around the village streets, behind her spectacular bosom, defying those idiotic eyes jumping through the windows and yards of nearby houses. Due to her eyes, hearts were widowed and lovers babbled in deep mountain slopes. Her lips were a plunging fire, sweeping Adam in his quiet Eden. Was God too far away at that time? Even she didn't know. He might have been one of those with eyes absorbed in her buttocks, or under the wall of that courtyard from where a deep sigh emerged, when she bent to pick up her purse. However, God stayed far away, hidden behind the bleak dense clouds in stormy winters. He was the one throwing terrible lightning, thundering in his great almighty voice, saying:

"Here I am, O ye frightened people!"

Yet in summer, when the ground breathed sighs of love and freedom, God's voice fades away, disappearing with the last fleeing black cloud. She rushes to the sleepy land, sinking into its sighs, embracing its soil, wrapped in its green foliage so they would blossom again. There, behind the small knolls, by a drowsy creek flowing over sandy soil filled with gravel, Selim saw her embracing the strange youth. Both were naked. That day his eyes protruded and his ears were strained, while he shoved his head between the thorny weeds, listening to those strange moans mingling with the creek's burble, releasing a wild melody that moistly penetrated his body, making him snatch a green twig, indifferent to its thorns scratching him. He'd fled, startled, running back to his friends who were waiting for him.

Did she know? He didn't know for sure but he felt connected to her with a special bond no one knew about. His relationship with her was transformed into one of great kindness and love. She no longer refused him those small demands he was keen on, nor did she ever forget to take him daily to the village shop, to buy him the sweets he loved.

Moreover, she has become his permanent protector in the face of those who would dare refuse his small whims. A deep bond grew between them. She too, with her large, guilty black eyes, was aware of the secret, for the secret is not a secret if no one knows about it.

He was still a kid at the time, not older than ten but he was able to understand those sighs she emitted, when she went beyond those hills, to lie down on the bank of the small creek. Even years later, sighs continued to span the place and fascinate his fading soul until ...

Until she returned on that terrible day, that dire day when the sky was shrouded in ominous black clouds. She returned with her clothes torn, stained with mud and water, her Kohl[7] ruined, running in oily stains from the corner of her eyes to her chin, face pale and stiff like the dead. All night she shed hot tears on her mother's chest, delirious, muttering strange words about unknown things, whilst her poor lamenting mother cradled her in her arms.

She stayed in that condition for several days, sticking her face in her hands and squeezing the pain in her body. No one knew how God appeared that evening and retaliated. How He cast His curses on this lost spirit that dared forsake Him, nor how He thundered in that deep voice which split heaven and destroyed the masts of distant ships. Nor how that pale wax statue materialized, the one people saw in front of her as she worshiped and kissed its shadow. Yet, it was not the only thing that surprised them, for here was something else that led some to fall down in prostration before her. It was the sudden, intense gray that had invaded her hair, along with the yellowing of her now extremely gaunt face and glances from those dark eyes, which seemed to pierce directly into your soul.

There were lots of widespread rumors until they finally settled on the story told by one man. He claimed to have seen her exposed to this strange beam, which split the sky, issuing a great thunderous sound, making him fall down to the ground and bury his head in the dirt. However, some continued to believe her to be mad. Her life suddenly became desolate. She was always alone, by herself. She ceased to visit the creek and the good land, except for that spot behind a nearby shrine. There, she would carry a bouquet of white flowers that she would place on the bare, red soil. She would remain there until nightfall, in her studded lilac dress, before returning silently, her face shining strangely.

She listened without taking her eyes off his cloudy eyes. He confessed to her what lies hidden under his skin and bones, his voice scattered like frightened wintery clouds, his heart a pile of blossoms ruthlessly trampled under cruel feet. His eyes fled far away without quenching their thirst. He stopped a while as he wiped his forehead with his large hand, waiting for what she would say but she remained silent. So, he said disjointedly:

"But I love her aunty, I love her and now I have told you everything. What can I do?"

She looked into his eyes for a moment, then turned to her statue silently, as if consulting it. He remained silent, waiting for her words, begging with his hand grabbing hers, resting his head on her shoulder.

"Speak, aunty, why do you keep silent?" He demanded, fed up with the continuing silence. She tightened her hold on his hand and turned her face toward him, saying in a sad tone:

"My dear you are driving yourself towards misery. Stay away from her Selim. She is married and has children but you, you will have many other women."

"No, aunty, don't say so, I didn't come to you for this! I love her."

"I know. You have come for encouragement, for help but you are reaching for the impossible. I see in your eyes that terrible fate; the one, which befell myself. Here, you are thrown into the misery of slavery, you poor child. What can I do? Go to her my dear. She loves you. She sent you away because she loves, because she is afraid for you from herself and her destiny."

"She really loves me? Is it true, aunty?"

"Yes, my dear, she is looking for herself in you. Go to her."

"Thank you, aunty, thank you. You've given me a new lease to life."

He jumped up, almost crying from his excessive happiness, his heart crooning a drunken, joyful melody.

"I will go to her immediately, I will go." He cried, rushing out, ravaged by the fevered desire to meet her. The night had become deeply dark outside and a light warm wind blew, touching his face gently. He felt a cheerful elation permeate his veins. His feet barely touched the ground while he was trotting towards her house. His narrowing eyes were turning towards the distant porch, while his heart beat wildly. Inside him, a battle raged between mad fear and freedom. He was aware of the great difficulty he would face just to meet her. So, he started sharpening his courage, which began to fade when he passed the last house separating him from her home:

"What am I doing? Am I crazy? Oh my God, why did I listen to this madwoman? She is mad; she does not know what she is saying!" He whispered to himself, looking towards a lit window in her home. He knew she was alone there, until the return of her husband. "And what am I to say to her? 'My aunt told me that you love me!' Oh, I must be crazy!" He passed the porch and started walking along the street, feeling lost. He didn't have much confidence in his aunt after she was struck by this strange condition; madness and genius are unreasonably alike.

She had bewitched him with her deep fixed looks, leaking into his soul and mind with this mighty force. Yet, she remained with her vague weird behavior, closer to madness than to a normal human being. She often spoke to invisible people, laughing with them, arguing with them in unintelligible words and even sometimes in animal sounds, rather than human ones.

'Yet, sometimes she turns out to be true. She knows lots of things that nobody else knows.' He thought, summoning his courage before reaching the end of the road and turning to his house. 'How many times was she able to read my thoughts before I spoke a word? Maybe she is telling the truth!' Shouted a distant voice in his head and he faltered a little, then turned back around, his steps accelerated as his head became drunk with the fever of meeting.

"I love you! I worship you!" His trembling lips muttered. He stopped in front of the lit window, leaning on the stone wall of her house, his lips whispering: "Julia .. Julia, I came to you, I came because I love you."

He bent slightly; picking up a small pebble then, gathered his courage and threw it at the window glass. He waited, a little hunched under the wall, so that he can see her without her seeing him but no one showed. He picked up another pebble and threw it at the window more strongly, which made a loud clatter, making him prepare to flee. However, a few moments later, Julia's face appeared, searching with her eyes for its source. He jumped towards her, saying in something of a whisper:

"Julia .. Julia, it's me."

"Who are you?" She said, widening her eyes, trying to see his features.

"It's me, Selim."

"Selim! What do you want?"

"I came to see you, Julia. I know you love me as I love you but you drive me away, because you think without this I will be miserable. No, Julia, no! I love you and I will be wretched all my life if you stay away from me. I came for this. I came to tell you I am ready for everything, for your sake."

"Oh you are crazy! What has come into your head, are you drunk? Come on, go home and rest."

"No! I am not crazy, or drunk! I do love you; do not pretend otherwise, Julia. If we stay like this, we will both be miserable. I repeat to you, I will be miserable throughout my life if you leave me."

"Oh my God, what happened to you this evening? Do you

want me to cry out to my husband to discipline you?"

"No, you will not. I know. You do not want to. You love me."

She stopped a little, looking at that black ghost leaning with his hands on the walls of the fence, with his scattered intermittent voice.

"Go back home, Selim. Enough adolescence." She said this, disappearing inside and switching off the light.

He waited a while, then he staggered back across the street, his head bowed by the weight of disappointment, listening to the bray of contempt buzzing in his ears.

He kept chasing her with his stubborn confused gazes, waiting for her rapid intermittent laughter in her neighbors' yards, until he ran into her, alone in one of the village orchards. She sat by herself, watching the remnants of her cigarette smoke dissipate in front of her face. He hesitated slightly, as he watched those deep eyes wrapped within a cloud, searching for the unknown. His presence there was a coincidence. He never imagined showing her his face after that disastrous night. He had started to feel the size of his humility, while he pleaded for that impossible love. It was enough for him to live his dream, listening to her voice, or stealing looks of her eyes and her smile, without her seeing him.

He stood in front of her red-handed, feeling this death that attacks as suddenly as a giant eagle, plunging to the ground in its shadow and sweeping its prey up with treacherous claws. He turned suddenly around, trying to escape from her burning eyes. However, he was barely a few steps away when he heard something that seemed to him like a deep buzz, arresting his attention; so the muscles of his body stopped and his head seemed covered with a velvet cloud.

"Selim."

He turned around towards her, sluggishly, staring at that mouth smiling quietly.

"Come, Selim."

He hesitated a little and then advanced towards her slowly, trying to search for the secret of her eyes, absent in far away clouds.

"Sit down beside me."

She felt his hesitation and fear and she said, somewhat cheerfully: "Come on sit down, are you afraid of me now? Oh you are crazy! You come on dark nights and knock on women's windows, then return to me playing a role of the self-conscious."

"I'm sorry, this happened against my will. I swear to you that I met you today by chance. If you hadn't called me, I would have returned by now."

"Sit down; I want to talk a little bit. I feel a fatal emptiness and I am looking for someone to speak with."

Selim sat on a rock near her, bowing his head.

"When are you leaving, Selim?"

"In a week."

"Will you visit the village often?"

"I don't think so .. I will look for another life."

"Do you like the city?"

"I don't know yet but it has enough magic to make me enjoy its novelty."

"And the village?" She said, looking at him from under heavy lids. He felt the warmth of her eyes lashing his face with a hesitant, sad flame. He looked up to her until their eyes met; something dry, inert, was clotted on his lips. He remained silent, tied to her eyes.

"Don't you want to visit friends?"

"Perhaps, those who wish to see me."

"Who?"

"My family."

"Only?"

"Perhaps some friends as well."

"And Salwa?"

"No .." He said harshly, grinding the dry red soil in front of him, in his hand.

"Another one?"

He did not answer. The silence fastened between them like a nihilistic block of ice. His heart beat strongly in his ears and his eyes wandered beyond the ripe apricot bushes. She lit a cigarette for herself and released its smoke, straying away with her eyes. He felt his need to smoke a cigarette, so he took one from her case and lit it, stealing glances to her transparent smooth face. A heavy colorless object seemed to settle between them, beating like jelly between their eyes. He felt a shortness of air when picking up her nearby breathing and distant things gathered in front of him; a marble block with disintegrated angles. He hummed while clutching at a nearby branch, wanting to stand but her hand suddenly rested on his shoulder. She came back to him with her eyes, saying:

"Stay Selim."

"But someone might see us here, what would they think of you? No, I have to leave you."

"It doesn't matter, please stay!"

He looked into her beseeching eyes, drowned in a faraway dream. The silence of the air trembled inside him.

"Do you love me, Selim?"

" ... "

"Do you still want to say those words that you said earlier?"

"Ah ... I don't know what to say .. Please .. Don't!"

"Answer me, honestly."

"O... Om Saeed, I don't see .."

"Julia."

"O... Mrs. Julia, I .."

"Julia, only."

"Oh .."

She picked up his hand with both of hers. Then, she raised it to her mouth and kissed it.

The air was suddenly empty .. Lava from hundreds of volcanoes erupted. The remains of the universe fell in stars of fire across the heavens. Something fell on his chest.

"I adore you."

Its echoes reverberate out into space and then returned to his truth, hesitantly, distraught.

"I adore you." He repeated it, embracing her hands gently, kissing those branches of hot veins. Something like crucifixion happened with a clank. Something similar to the rebellion against death, on the threshold of the angry hell held him in its grasp. Anxiety in the womb invades every departure and she remained the womb of all those leaving.

*   *   *

3

I left him sunk in his chair; God only knows what he thought. His looks revealed what was inside him. He hates me; he thinks I am the reason. Why would I do that? She was going to die sooner, or later. Several months had passed since her illness; her body had withered through age and disease. Even if cured, she could never have reverted back to being a young woman; the whiteness of her hair had intensified and her face was heavily wrinkled. She knew it, that's why she tried to stay under her cover, not permitting anyone to touch her.

*

"Listen Georgette, I might not have much time left to me but I don't want him to be miserable after my death. I would like him to go back to his life, to his youth, he has suffered a lot .."

"Why are you talking in this tone? You are very pessimistic. My brother has assured me that the illness is insignificant, a bit of good nutrition and rest, then you will revert back as good as new."

"I am talking about Selim!" She said in a dry tone.

"Selim! What's up with him?"

She looked at me skeptically and then she said, lowering her eyes: "I know."

"What do you know?"

"No need for denial, I know you well."

"No need for drivel."

"I am not driveling. I am begging you to leave him alone."

"But he is not a child."

"Leave him for Rola, she will know how to make him happy."

"But she .."

"No need to get back into this. Do you promise me?"

"To do what?"

"To leave him."

"I! .. All right … but I will not stop him if he wants me."

"He won't want you, you just leave him."

Poor woman, she remained until the end, considering him a child. She might have been somewhat correct; he really was eccentric. He would lie curved in a ball in my bed like a child, refusing to let go of my nipple. As for me, I laughed at his behavior, caressing his hair while he fell asleep, without leaving my breasts.

Suddenly, he was standing at my door, for the first time he visits me in my house. I was alone preparing dinner after my brother and his wife had gone out.

"Welcome, Welcome, Selim." I said, trying to hide my surprise. I took him into the sitting room and he seemed confused, his face showing signs of severe exhaustion.

"How did you come by this way?"[8]

"She has not returned in a week." He murmured, staring into my eyes.

"Ah, not back yet! She told me that she would only be gone for five days."

"She wants to leave me."

"How! Who told you this?"

"She did. All her actions suggest this. She deliberately goes out for long periods and when she returns, she closes the door to her room."

"Really! How unjust!"

I knew that. She had told me that she couldn't take it anymore. He had to accept the fait accompli. He had surprised me that day. His face did not show the usual signs of hatred and resentment, which I was used to; this time they only showed a rather imploring confusion. I didn't know why he hated me, rejecting all my attempts at courtship. One day, Julia even told me that he'd said he didn't want to see me and tried to persuade her to give up my friendship.

*

I felt his looks penetrating my body and then, return to sink into a mysterious void. So, I took his hand and told him:

"Come, let's dance."

We were in the restaurant of a hotel. I'd invited them for my birthday. He didn't say anything but walked with me towards the dance floor, like someone walking in a vacuum. I felt his hand pressing my naked back and then feeling my buttocks while we were dancing, his eyes wandering over my neck and half naked breasts. I can't say I didn't want him; the mystery in his eyes often beguiled me. His wide eyes and athletic body made me want him to be mine, if only for one night. It was a great opportunity; I started to caress his neck and his hair. He seemed to be still hanging in the void, his face completely separated from the rest of his body. I threw my head on his chest deliberately, so his face would sink in my hair but he suddenly loosened his hands, pushed me from him as if he was stung, saying:

"I am tired, let's go back."

His eyes were malicious, burning with anger. He remained silent throughout the evening, staring into the void after Julia refused his suggestion to return home, saying somewhat resentfully:

"How eccentric you are! Why should we spoil such a beautiful evening?"

His took his glass and sipped from it without saying anything, looking submissively at Julia.

*

When he came to me that day, I did not dare woo him. I gave him dinner and then we drank tea while talking about Julia, until after one o'clock a.m. but he did not leave. Drowsiness began to creep into my eyes, so I started yawning in an attempt to show him that I'm tired. He said, as he contemplated my sluggish motion:

"I want to sleep here. I feel upset."

"Here! But what will Julia think!?"

"Julia has been absent for a week." He said in annoyance, extinguishing his cigarette violently.

"All right, you can stay; I have a room for you."

I took him to his room and went to my bed in the next room. The night was never as fretfully loud with physical need, as it was at that time. Everything in him said he would come; his anxious trembling hands as they held the cup of tea, his strained fingers caressing his cigarette, which he sucked with blatant lust, his feverish eyes with that brilliant glare.

I stayed waiting for him, counting the long seconds while they stumbled on my watch, until he came and silently curved his body beside me. I pressed his head to my breast and started to caress his neck and head, cautiously. He was totally motionless. When I called to him, he did not answer, he was sound asleep. His visits were repeated; he would suddenly come with the same empty, exhausted eyes filled with hope and entreaty. He would slip into my bed until the morning, when I would wake to his fuss while he got dressed. He would suddenly shift away to cover himself when he felt me wake, then rush out, throwing these annoyed looks full of hate.

I did not like this sexual ritual at the beginning but later on, I started to await his visits impatiently. On the nights when he was absent, I would struggle with my insomnia for a long time, before sleep flowed in my blood and I would give in to the arms of Morpheus. He had become a necessity, like essential sleep fixtures; the bed, the pillow, the cover and Selim.

Well, I had to buy a pack of cigarettes. I had finished my pack and I felt a strong need to smoke. I stopped in front of a small shop on the edge of the street; I bought two packs, after I remembered that he might need one too. It seemed to me the street was unusually quiet and the air more sticky. I crossed the almost empty street towards the nearby café. I sat down at one of the empty tables scattered on the sidewalk, shaded by a bright orange umbrella.

One of the waiters brought me a cup of coffee and a small dessert. I started drinking my coffee after I lit my cigarette, without touching the dessert. I felt I would throw-up if I ate it. I had a strong need for something bitter that was not contaminated with sticky sweetness. Then, this crazy adolescent appeared with his motorcycle hitting nearby tables, which led to someone stumbling and falling onto my table. A great fuss and shouting arose between the café's owner and the motorcycle driver, with a crowd of passers-by and customers gathering around them, making me feel chokingly besieged. I immediately took a taxi. I had to change my clothes that were stained by coffee. I could do nothing but accept his regrets when he'd regained his balance and started to apologize, very politely.

I was shocked by the frightening stillness that shrouded my apartment. Even though I was used to its emptiness, today it felt pervaded by the smell of death. I hastened to the radio without being interested in any particular program, only noise could remove this heavy block that lay upon my chest.

As soon as I started changing my clothes, I was suffused by a desire for nudity. Nudity made me sense my own purity, so I resorted to it whenever I felt this sticky sinfulness take hold of my body. I started to contemplate my voluptuous body. I envy myself that body, although I had passed forty some time ago. Smoke, in such a mood, had a delicious taste after dipping your lips in some brandy. I blow my cigarette smoke with fast frequency, trying to form a small cloud to sink into, while languidly watching my body through the mirror. I was enjoying the dreamy fabric that smoke strings painted about my chest and neck.

When I began to wear my clothes again, I discovered that I'd expended more than three hours since I left him. So, I had to dress fast. I was a little delayed, trying to repair my make-up, which had become a little messy.

On the way back, I passed by the café. Everything was

quiet, the café had returned to its previous condition. The damaged chairs and tables were also removed and the permanent smile that sticks to the mouth of the owner of the café, had returned. The waiters' movements showed grace and geniality, as they came and went between crowded tables. I continued my way to where Julia was lying. The air was mild, softly gliding along my back and neck, titillating me while the light gray curtain was falling slowly upon the street. It was filled with pedestrians who had gathered on the sidewalk, observing a convoy of cars decorated with flowers, parading a just wedded bride and groom, on their way to their new home together.

I did not find Selim there, just some women who sat upon a few chairs talking quietly around Julia's body. I learned from one of them that the police had questioned Selim for some time and then left the house. As for Selim, he had entered into where Julia was lying. He'd stayed with her for more than an hour after he'd asked for the room to be emptied. Then, left the house with a small box under his arm.

* * *

4

A majestic, smoke filled night, circling cellars and then sneaking into the alleys in ruthless clouds of heavy gloom. The air catches the remnants of odors from the recently put out stoves. 'They're still awake.' He stopped afar, watching the illuminated windows. He fumbled for the dagger in his pocket and felt hot blood accumulating in his cheeks.

'I will throw my words in his face, crystal clear and sharp as a knife. Let what will be, happen. He knows no doubt, nothing left but to end the situation.'

He quickened his steps heading towards the entrance. Suddenly, barking noises rose and began to approach him, rapidly. He kicked a black dog, which approached him barking, so the other one retreated with increased barking. He wanted to enter the big gate, so the two small dogs rushed toward him, surrounding him without ceasing that scary, frenzied barking. When he tried to kick one of them again, he stumbled, falling into the viscous mud. Wide eyes shone from one of the nearby windows, observing the ghost floundering in the darkness. The eyes widened even more and then disappeared, only for two tougher eyes to show. They glowed for a moment, then began calling regularly repeated sounds. The two dogs retreated after that, growling in low voices.

By the time Selim captured his breath and started to remove the mud stains stuck to his pants, Abu Saeed was standing next to him, saying:

"What are you doing here at this time?"

Selim observed him hesitantly and then said in a faltering scarce voice:

"I came to you about something important."

"To me! In the middle of the night! When did you come back from Damascus? I didn't know you were back."

"This evening."

"Come in, let's see what you want." He said in a dry voice, preceding him into the living room. Selim followed.

"Sit down."

"I don't want to, I came to you about an urgent matter." Selim said as he felt his empty pocket. 'Oh, it must have fallen, damn!' He thought, while watching Abu Saeed's surprised eyes.

"All right, as you wish. Come on, tell me what is this important matter that you came for."

"I want her."

"What?!"

"I want her! Don't you hear?" He said in a quick dry tone, the roughness of his voice deliberate.

"Want what?!"

"Her, I love her, I can't live without her, I will marry her."

He responded, with his fist drawn in front of his face:

"Are you crazy, boy?!"

"No, you have to understand. Nothing will prevent me from doing the impossible for this. We love each other. No doubt you know, do not pretend ignorance."

"Pretend ignorance! .. What an idiot, you are still a child, how can you think so?"

"No, you still prevaricate, you know and prevaricate." Selim's eyes were hardened, while he focused them on Abu

Saeed's eyes, which were devoured by astonishment.

"You have to divorce her."

Abu Saeed froze and his eyes iced over with that dry, pink color: "Julia!"

"Of course, who else did you think? You have to divorce her immediately. Maybe this is the best solution for you and me. I don't think you would accept living with a woman who doesn't want you."

"Get out, you scoundrel! Get out!" He raised his hand threateningly but Selim's powerful hand seized his hand, strongly.

"I will go but you have to know that ..."

"I told you to get out, or I will kill you!"

"All right, I know how to force you to do it." He cried, turning to leave quickly after he saw Abu Saeed entering into a side room, his forehead sweating and the vein in his neck swollen in anger.

He stopped close to the house, listening attentively to the sounds of mixed screams. 'Oh my God! The monster will kill her. What have I done?' His head began to swell violently. 'I have to do something!' He heard the slamming of the metal gate and he secretly observed Abu Saeed's shadow progressing toward his brother's house. Selim picked up a big stick, which had been thrown onto the stone wall near him. He jogged through small alleyways that brought him to meet up with Abu Saeed, behind the village shop. He jumped over the wall yelling:

"Stand where you are, Abu Saeed. We are alone here. You have to divorce her, or else ..."

"You scoundrel, I know how to take care of you." He said it jumping towards him with his fists raised up in the air. Selim swung his big stick and struck him hard on his head, which began to pour with blood. Abu Saeed's cry was mixed with distant dogs barking, while he grasped his bloody head. Then he fell, staggering amid a pool of blood. Selim observed him, his hand stiffened on that cursed stick. Then, he quickly let it fall and disappeared into the darkness of the narrow alley.

* * *

5

As soon as the bell rang, we ran. She couldn't overtake me; I always arrived before her, poor girl! Her new shoes couldn't help her.

We passed the school wall and then ran along the pavement. It was crowded with other school students, who have gotten out before us but we overtook them, jostling at the crossroads of the street. She was still beside me, raising her small black bag to her chest and running without appearing to see me. She looked like a fool with her thin, bare legs. It would be better for her to wear pants, so no one would see her twig legs. Mom said: 'She is a girl and she must wear a dress' but it annoys her - I know it. When we play together, she can't put her knee on the ground as I do. A vegetable wagon suddenly blocked our way. I had to overtake it without leaving the pavement, this is the rule but the crazy girl overtook it before me, taking advantage of her nearness to the wall. So, she managed to get a few steps ahead of me. I sprinted to get next to her, then, returned to a slower speed. 'I wish she would give me the gun! What does she need it for?

She's a girl!' As she entered her home, she threw her bag on a chair next to the door. Then, turned and stuck her tongue out at me, laughing. So, I cried aloud:

"Hey stupid, I let you overtake me!"

She didn't answer, so I entered our house. My mother was sitting on the big couch. Next to her was a woman with short black hair, cut like a boy.

My mother said: "This is Reda, he's in the fourth grade."

The woman commented: "He has become a young man."

My mother asked: "Are you hungry?"

I answered: "Very!"

She responded: "The food is ready, you can eat."

I put my bag near the metal cupboard. Then, began to eat standing near the table.

The woman asked: "Can I count on you?"

My mother answered: "I don't know but we may send Reda."

The woman enquired: "But will they let him?"

My mother replied: "Let us try."

I ate a bit and got out quickly. 'She will send me somewhere.' I felt annoyed. 'Let her go instead!' I sat in the house yard near the pond, waiting for Salam. Soon she came, carrying her small gun.

I asked: "Will you give it to me? I will give you the horse."

She considered, then said: "No, the wagon."

I replied, forcefully: "The horse!"

She started to play with her gun, without accepting. I left her and began dragging the wagon. I put my stones on it and took it to the corner, where I began to build a house.

She said: "I will lend you the gun for the wagon."

I gave her the wagon and took the gun. I put it in my pants and started running around the pool. I would get it out and shoot, then return it to my pants.

She was dragging the wagon, after filling it with stones again. I approached her and pointed my gun at her, saying:

"Stop, crazy girl, or I will kill you!"

My mother suddenly appeared and demanded: "Kill

Whom?! Come here, I need you."

I answered: "Not now, I want to play."

She commanded: "Come now, you will play later."

I entered behind her. The woman was still sitting, smiling at me.

My mother said: "Listen, do you know the police station?"

I replied: "Yes, next to the Citadel."

She continued: "All right, you have to take these things to a prisoner there. Ask the policeman about him and tell him, 'I want to give him these things'."

I said: "Give them to me, I will take them and come back quickly."

The woman, who smiled permanently, commented: "You are smart, I want you to take him this message. But it should not be seen by anyone other than him, only him."

She gave me a small basket filled with food. I put the letter in the pocket of my pants, then, turned to go out.

My mother said: "Where to? Do you know his name?"

I realized: "His name! .. I don't know."

The woman replied: "Selim El-Radi."

My mother said: "What is his name?"

I answered: "Selim El-Radi."

She said: "All right go, don't be late."

I ran on the almost empty pavement. The basket was not heavy and when I got to the station, I started to climb the broad stairs. I knew the police station from earlier. I had been there before, when we'd broken the girls' school glass window and stolen the ball. The policeman spanked me harshly, after pulling my ears. I looked through the open door. It was the same policeman sitting behind a wooden table. How I hated his mustache, like a broom!

I said: "I want Selim El-Radi."

He replied: "Who?"

He seemed to me hard of hearing, so I repeated: "Selim El-Radi."

A voice sounding like a quern, emerged from the inside:

"Yes, yes, here! I am here!"

The policeman asked: "What do you want from him?"

I answered: "I want to give him this basket."

He queried: "From whom?"

I responded: "From my mother."

The quern voice said from the inside: "Let him come, Abu Essam. There is no need for this, you have terrified the boy."

I looked at him. His face was large with a black beard, jutting out from between two rows of the iron window.

The policeman said: "Give it to me; I will give it to him."

"No, my mom said to give it to him with my own hand."

The bearded man pleaded: "Let him enter Abu Essam. Consider it a visit. I will never forget it."

The policeman opened the gate and I entered.

He was scary. He scared me when he kissed my face. His beard was dirty, harsh like thorns.

He sat me on the only bed in the room. His room was dirty and cold. I looked over to the officer through the iron window. He was reading, so I slipped the letter in his hand. He took it quickly and hid it in his pocket.

I said: "She told me not to show it to anyone."

He replied: "You are smart. What is your name?"

"Reda."

"Whose son?"

"Baheya."

"And who is your father?"

"Saeed Hamdan."

"Ah, how is your father?"

"He is out of the country."

He looked through the small window above the bed with a smile. Then, asked:

"Is she at your house?"

"Yes, she is waiting for me with my mother."

"Can you take her something from me?"

I nodded: "Yes, give it to me."

He suddenly kissed me on the mouth and said: "Give her this kiss, on her mouth. Do not forget!"

His mouth was dirty and smelt bad. I pulled my head, trying to escape from his hands.

He said: "You will not forget, huh? Kiss her on her mouth. Do not tell anyone, this is our secret."

"I will, I will."

He gave me a new, yellow ten piasters[10] note and I left, running. I went into a nearby shop, bought sweet qdameh[11] and rushed to the house.

'I will give Salam some of it, if she allows me to keep the gun until tomorrow.' I thought, as I entered the house yard. Salam was still playing with the wagon.

I said: "Look what I've got."

She stopped, to look at the paper package in my hand.

"I will give you some of it, if you let me keep the gun with me 'til tomorrow."

She considered: "Half of it."

I said: "Tomorrow, until nighttime."

She nodded her agreement. Then, I then emptied half of it into her hands. I put the rest of the Qdameh in my pocket and entered the house. The woman was still sitting next to my mom. Her dress was raised above her knees. Her thighs were large and white.

My mother inquired: "Have you given him the things?"

The woman asked: "Have you given him the message?"

I answered: "Yes, I have entered his room and no one saw me when I gave him the message."

The woman said, smiling: "You are a great young man, you are smart, come close to me."

I came near to her and she pulled me to her chest and kissed me. She smelt good, I enjoyed her embrace.

My mother said: "Go and play now, take these ten piasters."

I took it and put it in my pocket, without going out.

I said: "He told me to bring you something."

The woman replied: "Give it to me."

"No, he said not to let anyone see me."

My mother intoned: "But surely not me."

"No, just her."

My mother smiled: "All right, how stubborn you are! Like your father, I will go out to get some water."

We stayed alone. I looked around ... there was no one. I embraced her head and kissed her on the mouth. Her mouth smelt good, better than my mother's mouth.

She said: "This is it?!"

"Yes."

She hugged me again and kissed my mouth, while holding me to her chest and then she kissed my face, several times. Her breasts were large, smelling of nut. Not like my mother; her breasts smelt like milk.

My mother came back, she said, smiling: "Have you finished Reda?"

The woman responded: "Come in, I got the message."

I left the woman and went out. Salam was sitting near the pond, nibbling sweets. I looked at her bare legs. They were not as ugly as I saw them earlier.

I said: "I will give you the wagon in exchange for the gun."

She looked at me nodding her head and then continued nibbling.

* * *

6

They were walking together, her hand tucked under his arm in a street crowded with all varieties of nameless faces. A rainbow of colors, jostling on both sides of the street, with bare heads. Faltering hands clasping sticky bodies with crowing lips, under noses revived by the smell of the sea. Eyes contaminated with fear, gibbering in various languages.

She is part of him and he is part of her. Two hearts spreading out into the distance, fleeing to a crazy promise of the sun. They had just come out of the cinema, among crowds scrambling in search of a gap to break through. She kept pressing his arm, laughing, dominated by a dallying mood.

"Did you see how they ran naked on the beach?!"

"It was an interesting scene."

"How I wish we could run together; cross the street and run up the beach. Look at this idiot, walking beside her without touching her. There is no doubt that they hunger for fun and yet, they fear each other."

She suddenly stopped next to the display list and looked at him with hungry eyes: "How about if you kiss me?"

"Kiss you!"

He stopped, stunned, focused on her face, then asked incredulously: "Here in the middle of the street?!"

"Yes, what do you fear? No one knows us here."

"But what will people say?"

"Let them say what they want."

"No, I can't, I can't, Julia." He said, his eyes pleading.

She looked at him, her eyes glowing with bouncing untamed glitter then, pointed with her hand, to a taxi. He climbed in behind her without saying anything. The car took them to a secluded spot on the beach. Darkness was a fuzzy twilight covering the sand; the wind blowing from the west was light and sleepy, caressing their faces, painting a magic love forest in their eyes.

Were they dreaming? Maybe! For magic is the ghost of the future and the struggle is eternal. The past hides the present and the present is the past's whip. The future is the magic of a whisper, passionate touch and lips closed in bewilderment ...

"Kiss me!" She whispered, begging while she sank into his eyes.

He observed the sandy beach. It was empty, drowning in a gray sleepy dimness, the sea relaxed, lulling quietly. He closed on her mouth, drinking her quivering lips, while he embraced her head with both his great hands.

"Kiss me! .." She whispered again, pressing his forearms.

He pressed his lips into her lips, caressing her neck and below her ears.

"Kiss me! ..." She howled like the wounded in his ears and a withered glitter budded in her eyes.

She took his head with both hands and started to eat him with her eyes, with her nose folded under his nose, with her body waving like a palm. She bit his nose gently, bit the milky teeth under his tongue and bit even his weary soul. She licked between one breeze and another, the remnants of a ruminative past.

"Let's run together."

She seized his hand and they went running. The beach was

serpentine and sandy, the darkness a restless shadow. She laughs and he laughs. The blood boils in her veins and the sea spray evaporates in his nostrils. She whispers and he whispers. She licks her lips and the air smacks his lips. She takes off her blouse and he takes off his shirt. Her breasts bounce free and he touches her bare breast. Her skirt wriggles on the dark sand and his face retreats to the darkness, saying:

"The place is not safe, Julia. Let's return home."

Her eyes glow with a hesitant fiery glitter, then fades behind high chuckles and she shouts: "Let whoever wants to, come."

"But why don't we go back?"

"Go back if you like."

She had become fully naked as she entered the water, hitting its clear rippled surface with her hands, laughing.

"It is cool. Come on, come on, ha, ha, ha .."

"Don't be crazy! I feel a movement amongst the reeds; don't expose us to mockery."

She threw water at him, continuing her playful laughter: "Come on, come on, there is no one, ha, ha, ha .. ha, ha, ha ..."

He listened a little to the whispers of the nearby bush, then tossed his clothes on the pile of her clothes and ran to her. As he tried to avoid the sting of the cold water that she threw at him, he stumbled and fell into the water at her feet. He stood up and took a turn throwing water at her. They frolicked for a long time, drowning in the abyss of searching for a lost happiness, which fear had made absent, behind the paths of long evenings.

When they felt tired, they returned to the dry sand and lay on their backs, next to one another.

"Give me a cigarette." She said, taking a breather. He pulled his shirt over, taking his pack from its breast pocket. He lit her a cigarette, then lit one for himself.

They sat in silence for a few minutes, smoking their cigarettes while watching the remnants of scattered lights from afar. Her naked body was caressing his body, while the wind floated around them. The fear that clung to him in the beginning disappeared, replaced by a desire to dally, which started to convert into a deep pain, bleeding in his chest. The call of the flesh began to dominate and the fuzzy whip to tickle his head. He threw the cigarette and turned to her. Her eyes were touring the twilight sky. He kissed her lips then started to caress her neck and her breasts. She watched him without making the slightest movement, except for a scant smile shaded with her sad eyes.

"No, not now, I don't want to." She said quietly, pushing his head away from her.

There was a pleading tremor in her voice that made him stiffen, looking at her face. It seemed dry, broken at the corners of her mouth and below her eyes. His eyes fell to her chest, her breasts sagged like withered fruits and her nipples were pale, framed by opaque shades of violet. That quivering appeal had disappeared from her eyes. Her warm breath was silent and darkness flowed into the distance. He returned to lying on his back, looking up to the sky, which had donned a transparent fabric with frizzy edges.

He always feared those moments, dreaded them; they would suddenly come to slap his face with their harsh palm and leave him in disjointed shreds.

"Let's go back to the house, I'm tired." He said as he watched the dark threads in front of him, while she silently ravaged the void.

"But I'm very hungry."

She looked at him, nailing him with exhausted looks that clung to his eyes, icy and unforgiving. She then got up and began to put on her clothes. When she turned and started to walk back, he was still struggling with his trousers that had suddenly tightened and clung to his feet. When he finished putting on his pants, she had walked away dozens of steps and he no longer saw her, except for flimsy shades. So, he thrust his feet inside his canvas shoes, hurriedly picked up his shirt and shouted after her:

"Wait for me a minute, don't hurry so."

She didn't answer; rather she went on without seeming to have heard his shout.

He caught up and walked next to her, panting as he continued to button up his shirt.

"I'm sorry; I didn't think that this would bother you. I won't return to this, ever. You can trust to it. I don't know why I am afraid of these places; they just look suspicious to me."

He was walking besides her, looking at her face every now and then. However, she remained rigid faced, neutral eyes swimming in the anonymous space.

He felt that he'd done something wrong, so he started trying to fix it: "Don't be angry Julia, I may have acted inappropriately, but I ..."

"Shut up please!" She interrupted him, stopping to look at him and then resumed walking, silently.

He walked next to her, silently. Just when he thought they were walking toward the street, she turned back to the sand and started to walk slowly. That gray void stretched in front of her like a vast plain on a wintery day. He had so much to say but her distant gaze held him where he was; silent, speculating between the wind and her.

"Did you really love me, Selim?"

Her voice slit the warm air, settling in his ears with a hurtful ring.

"Really! .. I don't know what to say...... but I know one definite thing; I need you like the air."

"Like the air!"

"Yes, I can't imagine an existence without you. I feel dread and perhaps, death..... but with you I feel safe."

"Do you fear death?"

"No....I don't think so. Maybe I am more afraid of life; life here is noisy and strange. I always feel threatened; their looks are greedy, voracious, even Georgette looks like them, I'm afraid of her."

"Afraid of Georgette! What a man you are. Don't you see how nice she is? If not for her help, we wouldn't have been able to manage so easily!"

"I am not talking about this; there is something scary in her kindness. Have you seen her voracious gaze? Even when she looks at a woman, it seems like she will eat her."

"Don't you think she is more beautiful than me?"

"No, never! You are far more beautiful than her."

"And her body? Does it not seem more attractive to you?"

"Er, why you are asking like this?" He said complaining, looking at her face and eyes, which remained fastened behind the shadows of the nearby city.

"Nothing, just an ordinary question!"

"Ordinary! No, I don't think so. You imagine that I want her."

"Really, you don't want her?"

"No, I hate her!" He said angrily, stopping to look at her and then he added with a less sharp tone:

"You have to understand this. I hate her and I do not want to see her, ever!"

"No need for that, Selim. You can do what you want. After all, we are only friends. We mustn't forget that we are not a married couple." She replied coldly, her relaxed smile, stiffened.

"Do not talk so, please; I don't want anyone but you. You know, I will not relax before we get married and have children."

"Children?!" Her eyes froze as she repeated this word.

"Of course, I want a son from you."

"No, this will never happen."

"Why?"

"I think we talked about this a lot before now."

"But I want us to stay together."

"We can continue together, without these things."

"Without children?"

"Yes, I don't want another child."

"But with me it will be something else."

"It seems I am tired, let's return." Her gaze hardened as she uttered her last sentence, so he had no choice but to follow her, silently. They crossed the bush and the railroad, until they arrived at the broad street. It seemed noisy and hot, its lights playing a ghostly silent tune, its colors withering into intermittent patches of gray.

"You go back home, I've got an appointment with Georgette."

"At such a time; it is past ten o'clock!" He said looking at his watch and complaining.

"We have work that we didn't finish."

She stopped a little, turning her gaze smilingly into his eyes. Then she said:

"If you want to see her, you can come with me."

There was something of a challenge in her last words, making his eyes burn with anger.

"No, you go to her alone." He retorted, stopping a taxi. He climbed in without saying goodbye to Julia, whose smile withered while she observed his testy movements. The driver gazed at his face, waiting to be informed of the destination required but he remained silent, lost in a trance, so he hastened to ask:

"Where to, sir?"

"Hamra[12]." He did not have any desire to return home alone, so he decided to amuse himself for a while, until Julia finished her work.

In Hamra Street, the night had fled from the din of colorful machines. He slipped his body between the nameless faces and started to walk. Things had a permanent mystique in this street; he had often extinguished his anger inside this whirlwind of colors and sounds. He would walk for hours here and there, exploring the eager shop windows, entrapping bodies and faces in astonished stares, immersed in long comparisons.

'That dress is adorable but not on her.' 'This transparent blouse is wonderful but with a burgundy skirt.' 'Those high heeled shoes would fit her feet better without socks.' 'But that silver color suits her skin more.' 'Oh, this woman looks like a monkey with this elegant blond young man!' When he reached those voracious nightclubs, he is stunned with the raucous image tampering with his eyes, so he turned back to the street itself.

On this evening, the air was heavier; he was not as charmed by things as in the past. The faces and bodies were themselves like stuffed toys. He stood before the billboard of the film they'd seen earlier. 'It's really a wonderful scene.' He mused, contemplating the image of the hero and heroine as they ran naked on the sandy beach, their shadows extended and retreating on the sand. He was invaded by an intense desire to see her, to return with her to the beach.

"How stupid of me!" He muttered, while still immersed in the picture. 'If I had not spoilt this happiness with my own stupidity!' He suddenly noticed a little girl regarding him with amazement, while grabbing her mother's hand. She seemed as if she was saying, 'Look at this crazy man.' He looked at his watch; it was a little past midnight. 'She might be waiting for me now.' He thought, while slipping through the crowd and taking a taxi to return home.

The car bypassed the narrow streets and settled on the broad highway. He took a cigarette and started to smoke. The highway was almost empty except for a few small cars, which passed by, or lagged behind them. Suddenly, his eyes leapt towards a car that had slightly passed them. He glimpsed Julia among a group of girls and they were laughing loudly. He fixed his eyes on the rear glass; the same hair, the same neck, the same blouse.

"It is her!" He murmured, causing the driver to look at him through his mirror with amazement.

"Can you get closer to that car? I think I saw a relative of mine and I want to make sure of that."

The young driver smiled, saying:

"As you wish, sir."

The car drove a bit closer, until it came alongside the other car but they had entered into a non-lighted section of the street, so he was unable to check her face. When that dark part was almost over, the other car suddenly veered towards a side street.

"Did you identify her, sir?" The driver asked, noting his agitation.

"No, I couldn't be sure; it was a dark street."

Later, when he started up the stairs toward her apartment, his agitation increased. 'She must be waiting for me, Oh, I am a wretch!' He reproached himself, while he turned the key to go in. The apartment was dark, so he turned on the light and entered the bedroom. It was empty. She was not home yet. He opened the window and stretched out on the bed, kicking off his shoes.

He noticed that he hadn't turned off the light, so he lazily got up, extinguished it and then returned to lie down. He tried to sleep but he couldn't. His head remained busy, swelling with images and ideas that kept bombarding him, successively. He remembered that the next day was a weekend, so he refrained from his desperate attempts. He took a look at his watch and found that it was past one thirty. There was no need to worry. It was not the first time that she'd remained at Georgette's. 'What a filthy woman!' He cried inside. He felt the blood rushing to his temples, so he threw his cover off and got up. He turned on the light and went to the toilet. He urinated noisily, then washed his hands and entered the kitchen.

He was assaulted by a sense of hunger, gnawing away at the pit of his stomach. He remembered that he'd not eaten since lunch. He ate two pieces of cheese without bread, then returned to the bedroom and stretched out again. He took a swig from a bottle of beer he'd brought with him. He kept it in his mouth for a while and then swallowed. He felt the beer flow in his throat and he put down the bottle and went out.

* * *

7

It was a beautiful day. We went to the cinema, after we'd wandered a bit in the streets. It was a boring film but Julia liked a scene in which the hero and heroine appear naked, as they run on the beach. True, there was some charm in the scene but other than that, the film tells the love story of teenagers who got married despite the opposition of their parents. An ordinary story we see a lot in real life, except that the director was able to bestow upon it a ray of a beauty, when he presented that scene.

After that we kept walking aimlessly in the street. She talked to me about this scene and said she wishes that I could kiss her. She surprised me with this wish of hers. It'd been a long time since she ceased those exotic whims of hers. How she scared me at the beginning; as soon as we crossed the borders coming to Lebanon, she'd turned into this frivolous, teenage girl. She would stop at every free, quiet opportunity, in order to bend towards me, kissing my face and discharging a cascade of mischievous laughter. In her eyes, there was that charming madness that will strip you of the remnants of resistance. She would sway in front of me, like a python just born, writhing its supple soft body amid the fragmented soil, in search of air. She would stop in front of shop windows, her gaze scattered over all the different types of goods, lit with different lights. Then, suddenly slip among the dense crowd that jammed the pavement, trying to tease me with her sudden disappearance. So, I panic and start to search for her until she finds me, having set up an ambush for me on one of the nearby corners. She would immediately hug me, kissing me between her long intermittent laughter.

They were really happy days. We stayed this way for more than two years. Oblivious to those distant memories that hid behind the towering mountains, whose snowy tops fused with the misty sky. That frivolous madness was transferred to me. I started to match her abundant frivolity, enjoying that renewed spring in her quivering body. I would slip my hand in her hand and we would run, laughing, unconcerned with eyes that devoured us with frosty extinguished stares, 'til we flung ourselves, breathlessly, onto those sandy beaches which surround Beirut. As soon as she regained her breath, she would hug me, attaching her lips to my lips, her eyes absent in a delicious dream, until ... until that cursed day came.

The atmosphere was suffocating in the house and boredom was sneaking in with the moist sea breeze. We decided to waste the day in the streets of the city, which remained a hidden shadow fleeing behind our eyes, like a garment made of water. The weather was sharp, the air laden with the wild sea roar. So, we took refuge in the café's that littered the pavements. We toured the back streets, searching for everything that had escaped us for two years. When we entered that alley of the unknown lover, we wrapped ourselves with the wandering wind, while we passed by them. Two lovers, with deserts of illusion consumed in their eyes, they whispered, embracing in a nearby street almost empty of passers-by. She stopped, pressing my arm and whispered:

"Kiss me!"

That profound, ingrained ghost was thundering in her eyes, floating around with transparent, hesitant doves. Madness seemed a loose moment of death, so the fragments of emptiness faded in my chest whilst kissing those quivering lips, feeling that rebellious current sneaking into my body, a forever spring passion. I suddenly pushed her away, when I was stung by an obscene word that someone threw and then others followed him, as they laughed. The street was filled with those hungry troubled eyes, scrambling towards the cynical clamor raised by a few young men whose faces were free from any sign of modesty. I pushed her in front of me, trying to escape as soon as possible but they went on with their bawdy clamor, without desisting from trailing us. The wounded glitter of her eyes penetrated my blood; my heart was polluted by the subdued silence. I didn't feel myself, except as I was beckoning a taxi that appeared in front of me, like a distraught dream. I pushed her into it and then I threw myself in next to her, pushing my numb face into my palms.

Since that time, madness warms my silence. Everything started to wither and die in the rushing of time. Even when her face would glow and those eyes rumble with the dream of madness, she would push me towards the slumbering open space in a mountainous forest, or a deserted beach. Yet, their bawdy clamor stayed in my ears, an eternal tingle wounding my silence, even in the wild deserted places.

My eyes iced over when she asked me to kiss her in that crowded street, so we took a taxi and we fled towards a beautiful, sandy beach. Darkness wrapped the beach, so we were able to have fun and swim naked. When we felt exhausted, we lay down for a while but then we soon dressed and returned.

Julia said: "I have an appointment with Georgette."

I looked at my watch in astonishment: "But it is past ten o'clock!"

"You can come with me if you want." She said, hinting to my desire to see Georgette, which made me angry. So, I took a taxi and went to Hamra Street. I wandered there until almost midnight. On my way back I thought I had seen her in a car, accompanied by some noisy girls, lost in wanton laughter.

She had not yet returned when I got home. So, I laid down trying to sleep but I couldn't. The scene returned to my imagination and refused to leave it. I had replaced the hero and ran with the young blonde actress, both of us naked, mischievous and having fun. Suddenly, Julia's face replaced her face, without altering the slim ripe body and then it was replaced by Georgette's face but the body thickened a bit. It looked like Georgette's body and then it disappeared rapidly, so Julia's face appeared in Georgette's body.

I threw the cover away, turned on the light and went to the toilet. I felt a strong desire to urinate. The urine came out strong and thick; unusually I had the desire to urinate standing, which enabled me to observe the string of urine rushing like a pressurized water sprinkler. I felt hungry after that, so I ate a few bites and returned to the bedroom, bringing along a small bottle of beer. I lay down on the bed and started to drink it. It did not taste palatable but Julia liked it, which forced me to join her.

I remembered that it was weekend the next day and I felt a great sense of relief. I could continue to stay up without my conscience reprimanding me. When I recalled the beach scene, I was suddenly overtaken by the memory of seeing a woman who looked like her in a car, accompanied by those wanton girls. How this scared me at that time! I was often disturbed by her making friends with her students. They would sometimes come with her to the house. They would behave as if she were their friend; they would forget the age difference. She considered this difference even less; dallying with them as a child. I could not participate; they were secondary grade girls.

One of them, a beautiful girl who showed signs of affluence, was constantly visiting us; Julia considered her the smartest among her students but she constantly annoyed me with her flippancy. She wouldn't stop asking questions about my relationship with Julia.

"Do you really love her?" She asked skeptically.

"Very much."

"But she is too old for you!"

"It doesn't matter, I love her and that's enough."

"How long have you both been together?"

"For more than five years."

"I think you are not older than twenty five?"

"A little bit older than that."

"And what about her, is she not almost twice as old?"

"No, not twice."

"Don't you think she has become too old?"

"No ... She is still a young woman; at least that's how I see her."

"It seems to me that you don't see very well."

"This is a relative matter."

"Really!" She said, smiling then added: "I think you sleep in two single beds."

"No, we sleep together!" I said with something of a rage.

"Can she still?"

"Can she still, what?"

"You know!" She said, smiling and pretending to be shy.

"I don't know anything."

"So, you sleep together?"

"How else do you want a married couple to sleep?"

"Of course, as you said, together." She attached a short laugh to her statement.

"Why do you ask?"

"So, I know."

"Why do you need to know?"

"Because I'm her friend."

"How can you to be her friend, when you're as young as her daughter?"

"Really! How can you be her husband?"

"An ordinary matter, we love each other."

"She will grow old soon and will no longer be able to keep

up with you."

"I think I will continue to love her. I'm madly in love with her."

"But I think you want a young woman."

"I don't think so, I'm happy as I am."

"No, I have seen how you look at Samar."

"She is kind; and I don't look in a bad manner."

"I don't say badly but with admiration."

"Maybe; she is smart and kind."

"So, you admire her?"

"I told you, because she is kind and smart!"

"Is it possible that this admiration will extend into love?"

"Miss, I only love my wife." I said impatiently; anger beginning to seep into my head.

She laughed uproariously, repeating and imitating my voice: "Ha, ha, ha ... Miss, I only love my wife ... ha, ha, ha ... I love my wife .. only, ha, ha, ha ... So why do you look at me like this? Do you think you are Don Juan?!"

"Please, Miss. Enough! No need for such jokes."

"I'm not joking; I've seen your sly looks." She stopped staring into my eyes, her own eyes widening and then she continued:

"Can you explain to me why you entered into the room while I was changing my clothes, last week?"

"I didn't know you were there, besides the room is mine. It's natural that I enter when I want to."

"Of course, especially when you know that a girl is changing her clothes."

"Never! You are a big cynic. No need for such statements."

"Maybe Julia would be upset if she knew about it."

"She will not believe you; she knows me very well."

"Maybe! We will see!"

Julia wasn't home when Rola had come to see her and when I told her that she wasn't; she said she'd wait for her. She wore a short summer dress, which exposed a bit of her breasts. She was not older than seventeen, a brunette with long hair and a figure that was noticeably tall and full. Her face was a bit rounded, out of which two foxy eyes emerged, which made your facial muscles contract in alertness, while her mouth smiled with the naivety of a virgin.

"You seem to be annoyed by my jokes."

"Maybe!"

"But I didn't want that."

"And yet, you tried to annoy me."

"I didn't mean to; I want us to stay friends."

"We will stay friends, if you stop annoying me."

"I'm sorry!" She said in a sad tone, contemplating a mural near the door. Then she added, without abandoning a mournful tone:

"But even so, I can't help but be surprised at this relationship."

"What relationship?"

"Your relationship with Julia."

"Miss, this is not a relationship, she is my wife!"

"Why don't you have children?"

"Here, we have returned to the series!"

"Please don't get angry. I just want to know why you don't have children."

"What do you want me to say?"

"The truth!"

"The truth! Very well, I'm barren!"

"No, you don't tell the truth. She is old and can't have children."

"Here you are, answering for me."

"I answer because I know."

"You know!"

"Of course, she told me."

"She told you that she couldn't have children?"

"No, not like that but in a different way. She said she doesn't want children."

"Does that mean that she can't have children?"

"There is no woman who doesn't love childbearing!

Besides that, her body has become flabby, not like her face appears, because she hides it with powder."

"I don't see this."

"You don't want to see."

"Very well, as you wish." I said impatiently, having become weary of this talk. This made her go silent, turning the pages of a book in front of her. Then she said, with a bit of coquetry:

"It seems that Julia will be late?"

"Maybe, I don't know for sure."

"The apartment is hot. What do you think, should we go out for a while?"

"No, I can't. I have to wait for Julia. Besides, I'm tired and I want to lie down for a bit."

"This means that I have to leave?"

"If you wish to do so."

She fell silent for a moment while she looked at her watch and then said:

"It seems to me that it's better to leave." Then she took her small purse and went out, after she added, sarcastically: "I wish you both good luck."

That evening, Julia returned tired. Rebel traces of mild wrinkles appeared on her face. She lay on the wide sofa to rest after climbing the stairs, of which she complained continuously. I was still affected by Rola's statements, so I complained to her about it. Julia smiled, saying:

"Don't bother about her. She's a little devil."

I looked at her in exasperation, while she was changing her clothes. Her breasts seemed empty and drooping, while her neck seemed like the trunk of an ancient tree whose roots sprout above dry cracked soil. I lowered my eyes while trying to remember how many times I had seen her totally nude; it was really very rare, she refused to undress in front of me. The few times that I saw her naked, it was only quick glimpses; as she was quick to cover herself, which made me furious, saying:

"But why?"

"I feel shy; I don't like any one to see me naked."

"But that's normal for us!"

"No please, I feel embarrassed."

Yet, I have seen her naked this day on the beach, despite the darkness that was hiding the minute details. I could have admired this body if I'd had illumination.

Even when I wanted to make love to her, it was only so that I could contemplate her body at my leisure.

I checked my watch and found it was past one thirty. I was suddenly overtaken by rage; she was very late today. 'What if I called Georgette, to make sure of her presence there? But what do I doubt? There is no reason for me to distrust but why not check on how she is doing? Maybe this would make her feel that I love and long for her.' I dressed and went out to a nearby kiosk. I picked up the telephone receiver, dialed and waited. 'What should I say?'

Maybe it was better to say that I would like to check on her, this is better.

"Hello, yes." A cheerful, female voice answered.

"I want Madame Georgette, please."

"Wait a minute."

I could hear sounds of loud music and bouts of wanton female laughter in the background. It seemed to me that I heard her laughter; 'I will ask Georgette to give me Julia immediately. Why not? I have to know.'

"Hello, who is it?" Her voice seemed elongated with something of irregularity.

"I am Selim."

"Selim! Ha, ha, ha ... and what is wrong with you Selim[13]?"

Her laughter cut through to the depth of my brain, feeling this painful irony.

"Give me Julia, please." I said, dryly.

"Julia! She is busy, sweetie."

"Busy! And doing what? Give her to me anyway. I want to talk to her."

"As you wish. I will see if she can."

She was drunk no doubt, her voice was lax and her laughter was easy and gushing. Music returned to roaring and laughter to dancing in my ears, like a wasps' nest.

"Yes, Selim, what is wrong with you?"

Her voice came as a wounding buzz amid the bustle of music and laughter, which suddenly seemed to rise in volume.

"I am worried about you, you are quite late. I only wanted to check you were OK."

"Today is Georgette's birthday and we wanted to celebrate it."

"But you never told me!"

"Oh, I forgot about it."

"Shall I come to accompany you home?"

"No, no need for that, I won't be much longer. You can sleep, it's late. Good night."

I put down the phone receiver and returned home. My head was burning with that strange glare, which clings to my temple when threads of control slip from my hands. I entered the apartment and sat down at a small table. I had to hurry before it was too late. I took a paper and began to write a letter to Soha, pleading with her to understand my position and to help us to convince her father to divorce Julia. It might have been a stupid idea but there was nothing else left for me. I had tried through a lot of channels but he remained stubborn. He refused to make any concession in this regard. I resorted to my brother Ahmed but he refused to answer my letter. I begged him to understand my position and to help me to redeem myself, his answer came with one of the drivers, 'Let him leave her and return!' 'Leave her! ... What a fool, after all this! He did not understand.'

Julia was not aware of this last attempt of mine. She had completely dismissed this issue and accepted the status quo. There was something in this indifference of hers that raised my fears; I wanted to marry her and the presence of a child was necessary.

I almost suffocate with my knowledge that she is

approaching the age after which she would not be able to have a baby. Soon, it may be too late. I finished my message, including all I could of hope, an elaborate explanation of our circumstances and a desire to forget the past. Then, I put it in a small envelope and had just started to write the address, when I heard Julia coming in. I hid the letter, trying to draw a light smile on my lips.

"You're still awake! I didn't expect that."

"I was waiting for you."

"But why? You could have avoided exhausting yourself."

She was talking with composure; she did not show the hypothetical effects of drunkenness. Yet, when I approached her, I smelt alcohol wafting from her mouth.

"I felt insomnia."

"You could have taken a sleeping pill. The bottle of pills is there, near the bed."

She stopped a moment, throwing a small white bundle that she had in her hand, on a chair. Then, she stretched her body, opening her hands to their capacity and closing her eyes. Yawning, she mumbled:

"I feel tired; I will have a bath before I sleep."

"You look exhausted, I will help you."

"No, no need for that. You go to bed and sleep."

"Do you not see yourself; you look about to fall down, I have to help you."

"I told you I would bath by myself!" She retorted testily, as she entered the bathroom and closed the door, locking it.

* * *

8

<< *There are things that can be seen even from a distance, or maybe things permeate us without regard to places and obstacles; delve into our eyes and then sink in the interior corridors of our consciousness, breaching our oversight. When we spring to shake off sleep dust from ourselves, it remains floating in our blood, to pounce on the prominent veins in our temples and say: "Behold, I am here!" We suddenly jump and look, we see the depth in the coming things and we see pleasure in its revelation, waving from afar as it sinks towards the setting sun. We rush, running towards it and when we get to where the evening dwells, we remain near the cliff waiting but .. when the last thread of it starts to slip, we firmly grasp it and go on to the abyss of impossible things.* >>

It was the first thing that appeared in front of his eyes,

amongst the many papers, scattered in front of him without regularity. His desire to know what it contained was keen. He opened the little box and emptied a pile of papers and small notebooks onto the floor. He began to read this sheet of paper, which was written in a hurried and hesitant handwriting. He read it again and stopped at the last sentence, << *and go on to the abyss of impossible things.* >>

'Is this her suicide message?'

He was looking for a supposed message that she left before her suicide; he searched the whole room, he looked in the table drawer, in the drawers of the locker, on the small table near the bed. He did not find anything. He asked Georgette, who was the first one to discover her death but she could not help him at all. There was nothing left for him except these papers she kept in this small box, without allowing him to read. Sometimes he would see her writing, poring over her papers with a strange compassion. He would ask her about them but she would answer in a dry, cold tone, saying:

"I'm preparing some lessons."

When he approached her one day, trying to explore what she was writing, she hid her papers quickly under a book that was near her, saying:

"I hope you leave me alone, I've got work."

"But why hide it?"

"I don't want anyone to see it."

"Even me?"

"This is a private thing; leave me please!"

He was overtaken with doubt. At the beginning, he thought she was writing a letter but to whom? His desire to see what she wrote intensified. She never told him that she corresponded with any of her relatives; she never even mentioned that she had relatives; or rather he did not ask her about them. He halted, confused by his own oversight. 'O God, how did this happen? I don't even know her family!' Her history, as far as he knew it, was related to her husband and her children. He knew almost nothing more than that. It seemed as if she was born and had always lived in his village. This had been enough for him before now: she is Abu Sa'eed's wife; she has three children; she is a French teacher whose rich husband had retired to the house. 'Really! And what more?' Emptiness returned to his eyes, tremulous with concern.

More than four years had passed while they were together. They had all passed by without him knowing anything about her personal history. His desire to know more about her deepened and he resolved to ask her that evening. He may well continue to ask her until the morning......

"Julia, did you realize that I don't know anything about your past life, except that you were born in Aleppo, married Abu Sa'eed there and that you stayed together until you came to the village."

"Really!"

"Yes, I don't even know where you grew up."

"In Aleppo."

"What did your father do before he died?"

"He was a merchant."

"And your mother?"

"Just an ordinary house wife."

"Is she from Aleppo?"

"Yeah."

"By chance I learnt that you don't have siblings!"

"Yes, that's true."

"Tell me something about your life before marriage."

"Nothing to mention, like any normal girl."

"Did you not have friends?"

"Of course, like any girl."

"Did you not have a relationship with someone before marriage?"

"Yes, it happened like any teenager."

"Tell me about that."

"What is the matter with you today? You're exhausting me with your questions. I'm tired and I want to sleep."

She turned her back to me, pretending to sleep.

During the next few days, he tried again to inquire about her past life but she grew annoyed with his questions, saying impatiently:

"Let me be, please! Why do you have to assault me with your continuous questions? How obnoxious you are, you've exhausted me!"

Little by little, he returned to his inattentiveness, satisfied with what he had. Yet, her papers continued to haunt his sleep. 'Why does she hide what she wrote from me? It must be something serious. Perhaps she is corresponding with someone!' His head began to buzz with hundreds of questions, 'Oh, what a fool I am! How did I miss that! She has been treating me coldly for a while. There must be someone else. I will search her papers!' He said to himself, determinedly.

Soon, he took advantage of her absence and tried to open the chest of drawers where she kept her papers but found it locked. He brought a small knife and started trying to open it. He had tried this when he misplaced the key of his drawer. It took only a few moments and then the drawer was opened. He took out a white rectangular box; yet, he found it closed and locked seamlessly, so he returned it back to its place, trying to close the drawer again. However, he could not, despite all the attempts he made. So, in the end he left it as it was, hoping that she would think she had forgotten to lock it. The next day, he found she fixed a special lock that he couldn't so easily undo, causing him to cancel the idea of searching her papers. However, his desire to read what she was writing continued to burn in him. Particularly whenever he saw her taking a pen and start writing with that deep mystery.

He picked up another paper and started to read:

"Maybe things taste salty but my passion for them did not end. When life is degraded to this aridity, salt becomes an

antidote to my soul. When spacious delusions flee from my hands, my body refuses to rest. The dream smells of truth but the illusion is the passionate love of the impossible. "

He stopped reading and let his gaze swim to her picture, which rested on a small table near the bed. She was smiling, with that mysterious sparkle in her eyes.

"And what is the 'impossible' you are talking about?" He said to the picture.

"Curse this mystery! Even in your death!"

He lit a cigarette and started to smoke while looking through the papers, until a little book fell into his hand. He started turning over its pages, reading a series of names and parallel numbers. It was a phone and address book; Georgette, the school, Rola, Samir, Georgette's brother, Nada, the French Cultural Center, a Chinese Restaurant and other names he didn't know ... He threw the small notebook aside, then picked up a big blue notebook decorated with quiet motifs. He turned over the first few pages and realized it was a diary. His eyes settled on a page dated 01. 01. 1973 and he started reading:

It was a wonderful night that we spent alone. He whispered in my ear his beautiful words, ones that I have not heard for such a long time. It made my spirit happy and young, what a charming man! He has returned to me what I have always missed. Long years have passed since his absence. Yet, through life's experience, he still emitted such unsurpassable warmth and grace. I have spent this day happy! Selim did not wake up until twelve o'clock; it seems he had drunk a lot.

When he woke up we ate together and then we went for a walk to the shore. The sea looked fantastic, with its roaring waves under the densely clouded sky. Selim seemed happy, caressing my hand with his large palm. In the evening, I danced with him for a little while and then I felt bored and tired; yesterday's echoes are still present in my body. I left him and entered my room to sleep. As I write these words, I think he is still watching a police serial.

01. 02. 1973

It was a rainy day in which I didn't dare to go out. I called Georgette who had just woken up. It seems that someone is next to her. I begged her to forgive me for my inability to come as promised.

01. 03. 1973

He does not seem to be able to really understand what I felt like. He remains buried in his obliviousness. I am counting on her too much; she is beautiful, young and she can make him happy. How I wish he would understand this! There are things that a woman like me cannot offer; our hearts are pumping at different speeds.

01. 04. 1973

I went to the cinema with Rola and Nada. It was a wonderful Indian movie but Rola did not like it. She said it made her lose her temper; she felt tears fill the lounge.

01. 05. 1973

It was my first day back at work after my small vacation. I was happy and jubilant. I explained the lessons in a cheerful mood, which prompted the students to ask me about embarrassing things. I answered their questions with some candor, which captivated them and made some of them dare to tell a few bawdy jokes!

01. 06. 1973
I feel tired and I want to sleep right now.

Selim took another cigarette from the pack thrown beside him; nervously lit it and then took the notebook and lay on the bed, continuing to flip its pages. The words condensed in front of him and he wanted to know more. He flipped over many pages without finding what would sate his intense desire to know and understand. Suddenly, he stopped as his eyes widened.

01. 15. 1973
I love him. I love him madly! Today, we ran naked on the beach, my hand lost in his lean hand. He pulled me, shouting, 'To the sea, to the sea.' We swam, then we went back to the sand. We lay there for a while, then we had to get dressed as the cold began to bite our bodies. I observed him a little this day, his body is still lithe; although he is ten years my senior, he seemed brighter than me, his eyes still shining with that rebellious sparkle that I have missed for a very long time, his white hair drifting lightly on his broad forehead. I wish we could stay together; I have promised him that I will manage my affairs quite soon. I do not want Selim to be shocked; he is a gentle young man, I have to urge him more. It seems that her desire has eased after he treated her with this wounding harshness.

His hand was a little strained and his chest palpitations intensified. Still, he continued flipping through the pages, reading quickly. His lips were lax and his breath quick and intermittent.

08. 09. 1973

Roger invited me to his house today. So I dealt with Selim as usual. I told him that I would stay with Georgette, as we have work we need to finish. It doesn't seem that he easily accepts these excuses but Georgette will cover up, if he calls me. In any case, I will try to convince Rola to come in my absence.

He threw the notebook and started searching among several other scattered notebooks. He fixed his eyes on the pages of one of them and started reading its first pages voraciously. Soon he stopped in front of a page the uppermost corner of which was dated, 05. 21. 1969.

*   *   *

9

It seemed to me that things were normal and quiet. Words were lax with widened outlets. All we can observe in this rubble turned to melted jelly, science, art, city smells, sounds of church bells, the history of what was said and what can be said, the coming years of war, even my gasps above her white sleepy face were fragmented in a deep abraded vacuum.

How can I keep this up while she has fallen asleep in another trip and I am still traveling in the same train, drinking in air and going on unknowing of what could be. My chest is a heavy block of cotton wool, soaked in mud and water. I murmur as I walk in the dormant streets of Beirut, a love song my grandmother sang in front of her unlit oven, while she cried, waiting for him.

Today I am the remnants of wine deposited in the deep amphora. Darkness warmed me and then departed behind the banks of the sun, stealing a magic garden and falling down into cellars of hot coals, in the basements of the truth. My eyes glance behind my shoulder, looking for her. She is the desire to fight and wearing the war hat, in her eyes, hundreds of cities are widowed and buried dunes fall asleep.

*

At the grave of my grandfather on that remote hill, my grandmother said one day, her eyes yearning to the far away:

"I was always waiting for him; before we got married, when he would sneak into our home and after our marriage, when he would vanish in winter snows behind the faraway mountains ... and when he would go to war, I remained waiting. But now ... it is he who waits ... I hear him sing my old waiting song."

I looked at her old face; tears were slowly flowing along its deep grooves. I was still a nine years old child, I don't know what prompted me to go to my grandfather's tomb, where wild grass grew and thickened like a small bush. I stood close to it, listening to the light wind; it seemed to me that the wind had a monotonous, soft voice. I went closer until I stood next to it. The wind continued to play its deep melody but gentle floating voices started to whisper in my ears. I bent, putting my ear on the soil of the grave and started listening. Little by little, the tune began to reach my ears in sad painful whimpers, along with a voice singing my grandmother's song. Extreme cold attacked my body and my face froze on the dry soil. I don't know how I was able to lift my legs and cross the thicket of thorns, which scratched me while I was jumping toward the road. Then, I ran non-stop until I got home. I threw myself on my grandmother's breast and screamed, out of breath:

"I have heard him! I have heard! He was singing!"

"Who was that Selim? ... What happened to you, were you touched by a jinni?"

"Yes! I have heard him, I went to his grave."

"Who?"

"My grandfather."

"Your grandfather!"

"Yes, he was singing as you sing."

" Ah, you devil, you have torn your clothes and injured yourself."

"It's true! I have heard him ... Don't you believe me?!"

"I believe you, I believe you, my son. But do not go there alone again; when you want to, we will go together." She said in a sad voice, while her eyes strayed beyond the cypress bushes that hung over our house gate.

*

I began to descend towards the sea, while I was still murmuring this sad song. I stopped singing when I noticed the wondering gaze of a young man who passed beside me, entering one of the buildings. I continued walking silently, trying to track those lights that were scattered from afar. I don't know what changed in her; she started to be away from home a lot. Her once blooming face, her eyes dispersing transparent glamour and her rosy cheeks brimming with simmering hot-blood when I kissed her welcome, had faded like morning dew. On the surface, everything looks deep and warm but little by little, the fever faded and the smile became trite:

"I am sorry; I have worked a lot today, I want to sleep."

After pushing away my hand resting on her neck, she entered the bedroom and lay down quickly. My eyes blinked at the closed door, I threw myself onto my chair and went to sleep with her image fixed in the depths of my mind.

Then, one day I could not withstand it, I kissed her frantically while I was caressing her neck. I wanted her with the entire defeated predatory devil in my chest, my wounds were releasing their wind and moaning. I turned that mysterious cold head, messing with the hair dispersed around her ears. She pushed me and fled from my hand, so I ran after her with my heart swollen and my eyes defeated. I hiss into her frightened face:

"Don't do that, Julia, Don't do that! You're killing me!"

"Leave me please, I cannot!"

"No, you are toying with me!"

I pick up that slender trembling body, dive into its curves and drown. Suddenly, she ceased resistance and relaxed her body. She kept looking at my eyes carelessly, while I was still caressing her and kissing her neck with the brutality of a rapist, until her cold blood leaked into my body and her empty eyes stung my own with their frost. I pushed her away from me and turned around to go out. I am no longer capable of seeing those sarcastic eyes, or that marble neck devoid of blood. Her body was lax to the point of death; I can no longer do it, everything in her has stabbed me. I rushed out to the street and began to walk aimlessly! 'What can I do? It does not seem that she will give in but has she really grown old as she says? Her body does not appear old. She lies. I know it. She is no more than forty-five years old, yet she claims that she is older than fifty. But why does she do so? Does she feel bored and want to leave me? But she could have if she wanted to; there is nothing that binds us to stop her. She has expressed her desire to leave me more than once but I have always held on to her like a sad dream, jumping to her face and begging, messing with her hair pleadingly, so she goes back to her smile, saying:

"We will continue together, as long as we can!"

The last time, however, she was quiet and serious, her voice coming out deep as if from a well:

"We have to say goodbye, Selim. There are things that a person cannot realize the essence of at the beginning but bit-by-bit, they invade the conscience and kill those who do not free themselves from their weight. You know, Selim that I am past fifty and you are still in the prime of your youth. You can chart your life anew; I am no longer capable of keeping up with you. We have to accept the status quo. Life is stronger than reckless desires; just open your eyes and you will see someone who will water your youth with hot blood and ..."

"No! .." I yelled at her, in panic.

"No, Julia, this will not happen, you cannot leave me! I do not want another woman, even if she were the most beautiful one in the world. Only you; it does not matter how old you are, I love you as you are."

"Calm down, Selim! You have to understand this; it is no longer possible to restore what has ended and ceased to be. I have to go out of your life, so you can continue without hindrance!"

"Hindrance! What are you talking about? ... Do not talk like this please, I am happy this way."

"But you have to understand!" She screamed at me, fed up with my breathless pleading words.

"I will not understand anything, we will stay together!" I said angrily, turning to go out to the balcony. I often fled from her when I could not defend myself, I would throw my decisive resolution and leave, preventing her from pursuing the discussion. Most of the time, my obstinacy paid off and made her return to calm me. However, that day she did not lift a finger, she remained static in her seat. In the following days she started her battle to convince me but not through discussion, rather through this coldness and indifference.

*

When I reached the broad highway parallel to the seaside, I crossed it toward the pier. The darkness had fallen and lights twinkled, shooting their colors across billboards. I stopped in front of a café, which had suddenly emerged in front of me like a magic genie blown out from his bottle; a nice building decorated with yellow stone, its three stories descending gradually towards the ocean. I entered the large room adjoining the pavement, looking for an empty table but the room was crowded. I couldn't find an empty place to sit, so I turned intending to leave but the debonair waiter attended me saying:

"Sir, please come on in, we have places on the first floor."

I followed him up the great spiral staircase that sat in the middle of the café, until we came to a small room surrounded by large windows. It was empty except for a small crowd gathered in a circle around two tables placed next to each other. I noticed traces of drunkenness on some of them as they were laughing and talking loudly. A balcony jutting out towards the sea caught my attention, so I immediately went towards it, saying to the waiter:

"Whiskey, please."

A few moments later, the table was covered with many dishes surrounding this golden, warm bottle. I started sipping from my full tumbler while contemplating the sea, which was gently lapping below the balcony. My eyes stretched to the lights of small fishing boats, glancing at the small noisy group from the periphery of my vision, from time to time. They were laughing with their eyes radiating honest joy, some of which splashed onto me, titillating my mind with a beautiful dream. There were five young men and three young women, who seemed to be in the prime of life. Yet, what attracted my eyes was this fifty-year-old woman who sat amongst them. She turned, from time to time, towards the girl and young man who were sitting either side of her, to kiss them alternately with a joy that seemed flagrant in her eyes and rosy cheeks. My eyes met hers suddenly, so I turned my eyes towards the sea and stretched my hands toward my tumbler, in confusion ...

I sipped a little and then lit a cigarette, while I watched the distant boats bobbing on the tide. Moments later, the group began singing, accompanied by a musician that played a skillful tune on a lute. I changed the position of my chair, so I could observe them without obscuring the view of the sea. A very tan young man began to sing with a beautiful voice. So, I listened to his song, contemplating the woman with her provincial clothes, as she sat amongst this group of playful young people in a café on the sea. This raised a lot of questions in my mind; my eyes kept watching this tolerant bright face, with its fascinating eyes and a nose that was a little bit large but did not mar that serene face above those soft, bemused lips.

Her eyes returned to pick up my eyes with strange compassion; there was something in her look, which seeped into my thoughts, teasing me gently. The lashes of her black eyes seemingly stretched to anoint my lips and my nose, making me feel a delicious itch on its tip but I did not scratch it. I froze in my place momentarily, then my eyes fled to where the sea babbled beyond the balcony.

A girl addressed everyone saying:

"Do you know that Om Samir has a great voice?"

Voices clamored for Om Samir to sing. She agreed, after shy objections. Her voice was really lovely. She started singing in a low voice, her face blushing in embarrassment. Then, gradually her voice began rising, singing an old country song that evoked distant visions which soon took flight. A modicum of sadness imparted her voice with an honesty, which made everyone listen whilst contemplating that Marion like face, which sank in the euphoria of permanent nostalgia. Her voice drowned in the whispers of the nearby sea, the night murmuring its longing. A light sea breeze accompanied the melody, as my lips chanted some of the ends of her song.

She did not stop catching my eye while singing and mine did not escape her. I feel a certain familiarity towards her, forgetting that I am on another table and that I am a stranger to them. I was so engaged with all my feelings in their joy and happiness, as they laughed around her in encouragement. When she finished, the young man near her embraced her and kissed her face but she did not pull away, rather she put her hand on his shoulder and whispered without leaving my eyes. The young man looked at me, smilingly and began to speak to the others in a low voice. Some turned around to me curiously, then the young man stood up and started moving towards me. He was headed towards me! 'What did he not want? I have not done anything.' My chest started to vibrate and my head glowed strongly, when he stopped in front of me, saying:

"Hello, sir."

"Hello." I said, in a low voice as I stood.

"You seem to be alone and I am celebrating my marriage as you can see. We'd like you to come and share our joy."

"Congratulations! In fact, I was sharing your joy and I would be happy to join you."

They were a nice set; his two sisters, his wife and his friends, a small family lovingly wrapped around the young couple. They welcomed me very warmly and did not leave me a chance for embarrassment; I found myself sharing their songs and laughter. I commended Om Samir's voice, saying that I hadn't heard a voice with such honesty and purity, since I'd left my village. As for her, she sat opposite me, trying her best to make me happy; whenever she felt I was fidgeting a little, she would interest me with her simple sweet words, while providing me with a glass, or extending a pack of cigarettes.

I spent nearly two hours with them and then left, making my excuses and wishing them continuous happiness. I shook their hands in goodbye but she insisted on escorting me to the outside door, without allowing me to pay my account. She watched me with her wonderful eyes, until I crossed the street and I waved my hand at her from afar, then began to climb the road to return home. Although I was reeling a little I didn't hail a taxi; the air seemed to me fresh and soft, the gray darkness granted me a liquid warmth that tickled my chest. Her voice was still in my ears, her eyes stroking my face, which felt the delicious touch of her eye lashes on my nose. I felt a bit choked with tears but I found escape in her song. I began to sing her song, her voice drowning out the voices and all the bustle of the street, her Marian face a vision, eclipsing the hustle and lights before me.

I walked alone, accompanied by sequential pictures of things long since gone; my brother Ahmed, his wife and their children, my mother who lives with her ghosts, my aunt and her permanent babbling, my other aunt, that tarnished saint ... My shoe caught on a stone and I stooped to pick it up, casting it aside whilst I continued walking and chanting in a whisper. When I arrived near my building's entrance, Julia's pale face, her freezing eyes, her stiff wooden body ... they all assaulted me. I turned back, sensing this hot uproar burning my ears.

The street was crowded with bodies, which where clumsily elongated. I sniffed the smell of burnt oil and my nose tensed. Georgette's image suddenly jumped out in front of me, with her full body and her intrusive, avaricious eyes .... I found myself knocking on her door. For the first time I visited her alone, although I had often brought Julia to her home, without entering myself.

She seemed to me vulgar, with a thief's eyes. She would invade my guts with those greedy eyes of hers; she would conquer me with confident laughter, while she toyed with her golden ring. Her smile filled me with fear as her eyes explored my face, or any part of my body, I wished the earth would split apart and swallow her up. Even my hand would start to tremble when she touched it with her piercing eyes.

Yet, today there was something dragging me to her; I could not resist her savage, bewildering appeal. A mighty hand led me towards her, something growling in my chest, pushing me to my death. I resisted with the remains of a stolen will but my body was taken over by the demon of the unknown, grabbing my neck.

I woke up the next morning and I was lying in her bed, my head pillowed on her great breasts, with the smell of milk filling my nose. She was still asleep when I jerked up from her bed and began to put on my clothes, quickly. A feeling of defilement filled my heart, while I was trying to cover my naked body from her thieving eyes. I didn't reply to the words that came out of her mouth without reaching my ears, I fled, leaving without even buttoning up my shirt. I cursed all alcoholic and non-alcoholic beverages. I shot my expletives towards my unknown enemy, then I made a promise to myself that I would never ever do this again. Yet, I woke up again the next week, to find myself in her bed and my head jammed between her breasts. I fled again and repeated my firm promise, only to wake again, naked, my face squeezed between her two breasts with their milky smell.

Julia did not change her attitude toward me; she started to increase her periods of her absence but without leaving me. The bedroom became hers alone, after she told me that I had to sleep in the other room. I did not submit, I clung to the bed angrily, begging but she remained all rigid faced and frozen eyes, saying:

"No, this will not happen anymore, you have to sleep in the other room."

"I will stay here!" I said sitting on the bed.

"Then I will sleep in the other room."

"We will stay together!" I shouted, as I forcibly held her wrist.

"Don't be a child!"

Her tense voice seared my ears, my face glowed intensely and I trembled with anger. I yelled at her, threateningly:

"I am not a child, Julia, stop playing your games! You will never belong to any one except me, do you understand?"

"I will not belong to anyone, except to whom I want!" She shrieked in defiance.

"So, there is someone else?"

She did not answer but glared at me challengingly, her face increasingly tight. I strongly pulled her wrist; she screamed in pain and then slapped my face hard.

Glass shattered in my head, exploding in the empty space

causing widening blast waves. It hurt my head and seeped into my consciousness.

I dropped her wrist, my hands leaping to cradle my face with their palms. I don't know how all that defiant anger melted, or how my tears fell on her hands as she touched my head gently, in apology. She rose to go to the other room. Then, with a look of strange compassion, which made me lie down on my bed quietly, she threw the cover over my relaxed body and left. I dozed quickly that night; it was a deep sleep, deeper than I had ever known before.

The next night she did not return. She remained absent for three consecutive days and when she returned, she was not alone. Rola was with her, lively as ever, with her dress sticking to her body like a glove, as she tried to dance with me. My eyes ran toward Julia, begging her to save me but she turned away smiling and entered the kitchen. Rola's body was wonderful inside that elegant dress, which stroked her thighs in harmony. Her voice had the hoarseness of a snake as she whispered in my face, saying:

"Ah! Why are you like that, Selim; don't you know how to dance?"

"No, Julia knows better than me."

"Do you want me to dance with Julia?" She said laughing, grabbing my hand.

"Come, I will teach you, don't be dull."

"I don't want to do this, dance alone."

"Hey you are wily, don't you see that this dance needs two dancers?!"

"Forget that, I would just love to watch you dance."

"Really? I will dance for you, if that's what you want."

My face glowed at her response. I didn't want that but I said it trying to evade her urgings.

She changed the record and started to dance solo. I sat on a nearby chair, contemplating her body coiling around like a sinuous snake, welcoming a spring overloaded with flowers. She sashayed towards me like a sleepy sun coming into view through her silky, transparent veil. She was swaying and laughing, kissing the air and laughing, drawing circles in the air and laughing, her body seemed like a toy laughing and I, I was still waiting for Julia. She had disappeared into the kitchen, which seemed to have swallowed her like a black hole.

"Julia, Julia....." I shouted, calling her: "Are you not bringing the coffee?"

Julia replied from the kitchen without coming out, saying: "I will bring it right away."

Rola had stopped dancing, her laughter dispersed and the glitter of her eyes vanquished. She sat on a chair beside me, saying with something of a hidden annoyance:

"You did not like my dancing, did you?"

"No, not at all, your dancing is beautiful. You are very ingenious but I feel a strong desire for coffee." I said firmly, trying to repair my position.

"Do you like coffee so much?"

"Very much!"

"I am good at making coffee, I will make it for you myself."

She entered the kitchen and then returned shortly, carrying the coffee tray. The coffee was delicious; so I praised it, drawing a smile that was stuck on my mouth, trying not to look boorish.

She spoke with Julia about issues related to her studies and then left. I stayed with Julia for a while as we watched a television series, until she left me and entered her room. I stayed 'til the series ended, then went to the bedroom. The door was locked from the inside, I called her but she did not answer, so I went back to my room in silence.

That day, she told me that she would be absent for several days and when I objected, she smiled saying:

"There is plenty of food in the kitchen, you will not need anything."

On the evening of that day, Rola came with her permanent book under her arm. When I told her that Julia was not here, she said smilingly:

"Very well, we can entertain each other for some time, you look lonely."

I did not object. She entered the sitting room, throwing herself on the broad sofa. She talked about issues related to the university and her friends, she said she was lonely and she loved frankness and clarity. She chattered about many things and I listened to her, pretending to be interested but she realized that I began to feel bored. So, she said all of a sudden, as if she remembered something important:

"How about a cup of coffee?"

"As you like, I will prepare it immediately."

"No, I am the one who will prepare it; you will love it, right?"

"Of course, of course, your coffee is delicious."

When we finished drinking the coffee, she suggested that we throw a small party; she will prepare dinner while I will go get the drinks. She said it without allowing me to object.

She was nice that day; she did not try to intrude on my life. She seemed tender and fresh as she whispered to me while we danced together, scattering her husky words about my face and smiling without vulgarity, she said:

"We can remain friends, you are very nice."

"Thank you."

"And handsome too; your eyes are calm and fascinating like the Beirut Sea at sundown."

My head was in her hands and she was playing with my hair while she locked her green eyes to my own. My body seemed to flow like a river, my chest felt as light as a feather, my heart beat loudly. She kissed my lips, her eyes delved deep into my befuddled mind. We lay down on the ground, which was covered with a thick carpet. Magic filled the air and desiccation decays in the deserts of my body and I drown ... She pillowed her head on my arm until the morning, then went out for a while and came back with bottles of soda to drink, saying:

"I will stay until Julia returns."

She stayed three days. She bloodied my body and tampered with my soul. The air was polluted, stretched and drowned while I scratched my body, which was blatantly afraid of swimming. She was a noise and an angry wind, she was a pile of cactus and its fluff was dispersed in the tip of my nose. Sinking and sinking, holding your breath and delirious but to no avail. She blocked my nose with the smell of popcorn and soda water, so I belched a violent wind.

During this time we went out a lot. We went to the sea, enjoying its whims. We climbed the mountain, which went up to Heaven; we lay down under its trees and defeated stubborn Gilgamesh, while we slept on the soil of his great cedars.

No sooner had she said goodbye, than the past headache returned to me; everything seemed to slip worthless through the door, clinging to her. The scent of popcorn and soda that pervaded her, like some luxury cinema. Those soft inviting lips, the gentle warmth of her tender belly, her smooth skin like a mirror's glass ... It all faded and the icy frost crept back into the garbage of my mind, biting my guts and extending its tongue to my lips, so I felt its dryness. My eyes are exhausted and my head abuzz with the noise of empty seashells. I pass through the busy streets, chasing my roaming ghost between their stores and when I wake up in the morning, I find myself naked, huddled in her autumn body. Georgette Nassor, the princess of incessant shadows, warms my neck with her breath. I sleep and sleep deeply, submitting to these warm breaths, seeping into my ears with her soothing words.

Rola continued to steal the fugitive moments, infiltrating into my peace of mind. She would empty her bustling absurdity, then leave me empty, awaiting fullness. It was as if I ate air bubbles, doing nothing but stimulating an empty stomach.

* * *

10

05. 21. 1966

My heart beat strongly that day; my body started trembling with strong winds that had faded long ago. Although, I found him burdensome at the beginning, yet still, his childish naïve eyes sneaked into my soul, shaking the remnants of a buried past. I don't know what to do but I cannot deter those scorching looks that he throws at me. I gave him a lesson today while resisting the voice of the dreamy gambler, warming present wounds with past whispers.

05. 27. 1966

My husband returned home in an angry mood this evening; he kept spewing his anger at my face, cursing things and names that I don't know. What a foolish, troublesome man! Mean even in his curses, his face turning into a red-hot mass when he loses his temper. Throughout our marriage, I have only heard news about his business figures; he rejoices but with a slight fear when he makes profit, his head falls in ruins and despair when subjected to any loss. His head and his spirit wandering between figures and goods, his eyes looking for a new profit and my body a losing number that he devours greedily.

05. 30. 1966

I don't know why that all of a sudden my heart dropped, while I was watching Soha coming on a run with her joyful eyes and her young body, which has begun to mature ... I run with my thoughts towards the future, while the voice of the past calls: 'There you are returning again! Here you go, losing again!' My spirit is redolent of the smell of heavy silence, while I hold her in my arms repeating to myself: 'There is no room for you, my baby girl in this vast world!'

06. 05. 1966

Selim came by this day, saluting. He was returning from the exam and had a lush smile on his mouth. He told me that he was able to answer the French language exam questions well enough. I congratulated him on that with a handshake but he kept my hand in his without stopping his sad pleading looks, while confusedly giving me words of thanks. I took back my hand, gently and then I withdrew, wishing him luck. I said to myself as I backed off from slight fear: 'Nothing conquers me like those childish, innocent eyes.'

06. 20. 1966

My soul explodes in search of life; in his eyes my eyes fall and dive away behind the sun of the hidden dream. Will I *respond to his fearful appeal? Do I whisper the remnants of madness? Oh what an idiot I am, imprisoned by confusion! I am afraid of him and for him, I wish I could escape! The wind noisily plays the melody of life; rocking my spirit like fear ... Will I be defeated?*

06. 21. 1966
I remained alone all through the day. I browsed through a picture magazine but soon threw it away, with the sands of boredom deposited in my mind. Something distraught and hidden was congealing in my soul, my eyes dry and defeated, my chest a burning mass of coals. I waited for him all day long. I remained sitting on the balcony, watching for his shy pleading eyes to rest upon me. I would have invited him today; I would have fled to him in stormy, devastating death. I would have thrown myself into the womb of madness. Yet, destiny was much more careful and he did not come.

06. 25. 1966
Today I went to the nearby orchards, accompanied by Soha. Soha turned around, saying with some joy, that Selim was sitting under a tree nearby. She asked me to invite him to accompany us but I strongly refused, pulling her hand and escaping from his eyes, which were burning my face with looks of shy anger. I decided that I would remove all hope from him. So, I hardened my eyes and froze my face, searching about for indications of angry grumblings.

07. 27. 1966
Selim came to me today, alleging his need for explanation of some tough sentences but everything in his eyes and moves,

betrayed him. I allowed him into the house laughing, dominated by a mischievous mood, perhaps, in order to hide my bustling, inner turmoil. I don't know how my will betrayed me, driving him to confess. He seemed like a belligerent child as he told me: 'I love you, yes I love you.' He flinched suddenly as if stung, dominated by an angry challenging mood, after I threw those mocking, sarcastic words back at him. All of this could have taken a new course except for that deep voice, which let me down with its painful lashes.

08. 30. 1966

What a scoundrel! He was a coward and he will continue to imagine that he can dispose of me, as he can dispose of his merchandise. I know how to make him yield, for he is nothing more than an empty drum. However, my nerves are tired to the point of exhaustion. I will take a sedative pill and sleep.

09. 05. 1966

I spent the day in nearby fields; I sat under an old oak tree, enjoying a gentle breeze while I read a French novel with a passion. After that I went back home to play with my kids for a while, then prepared dinner. After dinner I continued to read the novel in a serene mood, especially after learning that he will not be back today.

09. 07. 1966

Oh, what a dreary day. He suddenly came to me a short while ago, threw a small pebble at the glass of my window and when I looked down wonderingly, I found him calling to me, pleadingly. His voice was hesitant and soft, coming from behind the fence covered by the darkness of night. I could not convince him to stop, even though I threatened him. He kept casting forth his tormented words, indifferent to everything, so I closed the window and lay down, after I turned off the light. This was enough to make him return home but I remained troubled and don't know what I will do. He spoke today with a confidence that I was not used to. He said he knows that I love him and there is no need to hide it. From where does he know this? What a stubborn child.

09. 10. 1966

I know that although he makes sure I don't see him, his eyes are constantly pursuing me. As soon as I turn to him, his eyes flee the other way and get busy with something. It seems he is convinced with the futility of pursuing me with his love. Still, my chest does not stop throbbing, looking for him; he has come to sneak into my dreams like an oblivious destiny. His eyes have a strange glitter, which sneaks into my body like fresh breezes that make my chest tremble and blur my eyes into opaque, delicious visions.

09. 12. 1966

I went out with the children to the fields, we stayed there all day. A lot of joy flows to my soul between those wonderful things. They have become my permanent sanctuary; I flee to them when the dreams of a quiet life fade. My children are my only happiness in this hell; arid silence lies in all the corners of my worrisome life.

09. 20. 1966

What I feared happened. What I fled to and from, has occurred. Boredom had filled my chest with its great emptiness and insanity had filled my mind with the love of life, when he suddenly appeared in front of me. My eyes met his worried eyes, so I felt that trembling river permeating my body. The air seemed to have faded, while I whispered to him the remnants of fearful chills, which plunged between my ribs. The air stuttered between us, while the tips of his lips sank into my trembling, dangling lips. We stayed until the evening, gathering the scattered life to us; we sank in the dust of the earth covered with recently aged leaves.

I returned, wrapped in his ghost and my chest was jumping with happiness and euphoria. However, as soon as I crossed that door and saw his Lucifer barren face, my happiness returned to its old crypt, to be replaced by treacherous fear, stealing my rebellion. I do not know if I will go to him tomorrow. A deep angry voice is clinging to my head, crying: 'Do not return to this again, do not return!'

09. 26. 1966

Oh dear God, what can I do? It seems to me that I am caught in the stubborn mesh of life; I don't know how to get out of it! He no longer wants to part from me, something vague in his voice and his eyes warns me of a storm. He has surprised me today, by climbing up the wall of my house. He knocked on my window, calling me. I went down quickly to the garden, while I thanked God that there was no one with me. Shaking in anger, I rebuked him sharply for what he did and begged him not to do it again. However, he said with some regret that he couldn't wait patiently after I was late for today's date. I promised to come tomorrow and said goodbye with a kiss that made him leave happily. Still, if he continues like this, he will put me in trouble that I don't know how to get out of .... he is ready for any foolishness.

09. 29. 1966

I met Selim this morning. I had decided to end everything. I told him so, saying that what happened between us was just a passing whim and that there is no future for such a relationship. I am married and I have children. Besides, I am older than him by many years. I begged him to understand that he would leave the village in a few days, so we will not be able to do anything but part ways. He did not accept it; he said he doesn't believe in anything I have said; he insisted that we love each other and that this is enough for us. We parted after that in dispute, when I told him this is my final decision.

10. 05. 1966

I felt a great weight lifted off my chest when I heard that he had left the village. I thanked God very much, because I will be able to get back my peace of mind. Today, I played with my children as never before; I held them to my chest, sensing that supple, soft and warm flesh writhing on my neck. In the evening, I met my husband with a little fun, searching for the remains of humanity in him. Thus, I managed to make him cheerful and nice. Ah, I wish I could maintain this calm!

10. 18. 1966

I have wandered this morning in the nearby fields. It was a cold autumn morning and the wind was biting my bare neck. Boredom filled my chest and cold punctured my heart; since he left the village I've lived with his eyes, his smile and his confused words. I found myself in the place I used to meet him. I sat there with a reckless fatal storm messing with my spirit. My longing for him assaulted me, when I imagined that hurting sad face and those pleading eyes. I had decided not to answer his letter but today everything is calling me to a warm moment of love. I will write to him shortly, I will write my words, like any teenager, I want to live.

12. 31. 1966

He came to me carrying a bouquet of blossoms. He came at night without anyone knowing about his arrival. His head pillowed my arms like a child kissing my neck with that heedless frivolity, complaining from time to time but then he would return to his delicious dream afterwards. I couldn't stay with him long, for my family was waiting for me. He suddenly stopped me as I was getting ready to go, looking at me with this storm alert mystery, saying that we have to put a stop to this. I tried to explain to him the futility of that but he remained looking at me with that defiant insistence. His crazy stares make me lose my nerve; I don't know what he will do. I am sailing in a rough sea and I don't know where the storm will take me..

* * *

11

He woke up when the sun was already high in the sky; he often stayed up late at night before the weekend. His head was heavy; he was still tired. Lazily he removed the covers and got up, wonderingly. While he was crossing to the sink, dragging his towel, he glanced at her room and noted that her door was still closed.

When he finished washing his face, his head still felt heavy; so he entered the shower and let the cold water bathe his body, until he felt refreshed.

He returned to his room, naked and still drying his wet hair. When he finished dressing, his peered out of the window. The air was soft and fresh, caressing his face and neck. Suddenly, he felt a desire to go out.

He went to the kitchen and made coffee for himself and for her. He will wake her up, so they would drink the coffee together. A long time ago, they stopped this habit after different work schedules prevented them taking it together in the morning. She woke up early because she had to get to work before seven thirty, while he stayed asleep until eight o'clock, because his job did not begin until ten o'clock. Nowadays, morning coffee together was confined to weekends only.

He knocked on door quietly, saying:

"Coffee is ready, I am waiting for you, come on, don't be lazy ..."

He waited but she did not answer. He listened but didn't hear any movement inside. He knocked on the door again, more strongly. 'There doesn't seem to be anyone in there.' He thought while checking the door handle. On opening the door he realized that she had already gone out, her bed was elegantly made, her window was closed and the curtains were open. He looked at his watch and found that it was past the middle of the day, so he returned to his room, huddled and wrapped with severe disappointment.

He picked up a magazine near him and started to leaf through it. He sipped his coffee after he lit a cigarette, which he began to smoke with a sort of tension. He thought a bit about where he will spend his day, concluding that he will remain at home. It was then he noticed this small piece of white paper that was placed on a coffee table, in plain sight. He picked it up and proceeded to read it:

'Selim, I will be late today, do not wait for me.'

"Damn it!" He said, as he tore the paper into small bits and tossed them into a glass ashtray. Then he stubbed his cigarette out on the remains.

He relaxed in his seat, thinking about what he would do today. The door of her room was still open and he could see her large closet within. The hidden papers jumped into his head, for he knew they were there. 'Those damned papers that hide her secrets! That complex lock stands as an impregnable barrier.' It suddenly occurred to him: 'I can steal her keys and have a copy made while she is busy.' He calculated the distance and the time it would take and found that it was very possible.

He settled into this idea, brightened for a moment, then returned to his gloomy thoughts. He was disrupted from his dark reverie by the ringing of the outside bell. He looked to the door without standing, then muttered:

"Rola! Well, is it a coincidence that she came?!"

He went towards the door, running the usual scenario over in his mind.....he would open the door ready to embrace her, after she asks him in whisper:

"Is she here?"

With the negative response elicited, she will jump to hold to his neck and kiss his face, saying as always:

"Ah, how lucky I am, I came at the right time!"

She was standing as in the past but this time she did not ask him about Julia in a whisper, rather she said in a cheerful voice:

"Halo Selim, how are you doing?"

"Welcome Rola."

"I came to see Julia."

"Really!"

"Of course."

"But she went out."

"No, you're kidding."

"Not at all, she left me a message to tell me that she will be absent today."

"How did this happen? She has given me an appointment today!"

"Today?"

"Yeah."

"Well, you can come in; you have come at the right time."

"No, I couldn't do that, I have work."

"Yet, you will stay here today."

"You will force me?" She said coyly, while she kissed him.

"I will persuade you." He said, pulling her inside.

"So, there will be a case of rape in this place."

"Enough is this, Rola; you knew she wasn't here."

"No, I didn't know, I have come according to an appointment."

She sat on the wide sofa, slowly crossing her bare legs; her sexy pose deliberate. Half her thigh was revealed when her red plaid miniskirt receded. He sat opposite her, his legs open and his hands on his knees.

"Why do you come to me?" He asked her, with his head down.

"Because we are friends."

"Just friends?"

"And because I love you and I want you to be with me."

"Why do you love me?"

"Because I love you, I like you."

"Aren't you afraid of Julia?"

"No, she is old and doesn't frighten anyone."

"It is not like that; she might harm you when she finds out."

"I don't care."

"Don't you think she knows?" He said, staring into her eyes. She stopped for a moment, observing his face and then said somewhat coolly:

"I don't t think so."

"But don't you realize that she is absent when you think to come here?"

"Perhaps, but not always. Anyways, what do you mean?"

"She knows."

"I don't think so. Surely if she knew, she would have done, or said something to indicate that. Did she say anything to you?"

"No but let's assume that she knows and wants it this way."

"You're assuming something that's not possible."

"Possible sometimes, is it not?"

"I don't think so." She said, as she rearranged her skirt after she stretched her legs out and relaxed on the sofa cushion.

"But I assume so."

"Can't we do something other than talk about useless things? Don't you want to go out?" She said, as a frown appeared on her face.

Selim noted her discomfiture, so he said in a quiet tone:

"We can go out if you want to."

"Well, come on ..." She said, hurrying to stand and pick up her small black purse.

In the small café on the beach, her frown disappeared and she regained her vitality, boldness and perhaps, her insolence. She started to attack him with her questions:

"Do you love Julia?"

"I don't know."

"What do you like about her?"

"I don't know exactly but there is something which draws me to her."

"So, do you love her body?"

"No, I love her spirit."

"Do you make love to her soul?" She said chuckling, dominated by a playful mood.

"A person is not only flesh."

"Maybe ..... Will you stay together?" She returned to her quiet tone because she felt that she had annoyed him with her laughter.

"I think so."

"So, there are limits to our relationship?"

"Clear limits."

"Can't we become more than friends?"

"That doesn't seem possible to me."

"Are you really happy with her?"

"I need her."

"So you're not happy?"

"I'm not happy but I would be unhappy without her."

"Why?"

"I feel I am committed to her, forever."

"But she is not your wife. Besides, you sleep in two separate rooms."

"Who told you that?" He said with irritation.

"I don't need anyone to tell me so. It's clear from the way of life you live. Besides, her room remains locked, even when she is absent while you are sleeping in the other room and all your things are there." She threw her words testily, responding to his irritation.

"Enough fighting, why do we have to get into such details?"

"Maybe, because I love you."

"I don't call this love."

"Why, are you not happy with me?"

"I couldn't describe happiness that way."

"Then, why do you befriend me?"

"I don't know, maybe because she wants this?"

"Who?"

"Julia."

"And she told you so?"

"No, but I feel it's so."

"Why?"

"I don't know."

"What a man you are! It's as if you walk in your dreams!"

"Maybe….. I have been feeling for a long time as if I was living in a troublesome nightmare."

They both became silent. Selim began to deeply contemplate the sea, while she was drinking her glass, silently looking into his face. They spent some time together and then parted ways.

The night had drawn its black curtain and the street lamps were trying hard to dissipate some of the dark desolation, when he got out of the taxi and hurried home to his apartment. His yearning to see Julia was so great; Rola had opened wounds that he was trying to hide.

Over seven years had passed since they came together. In the past, it was her hope that they would get married. Yet, now that she had got a divorce from her husband, she dealt with the matter coldly, offering multiple excuses for her refusal. 'But why?' The voice of the past screamed in his head. Memories of their early times leapt to the forefront of his mind. The days when she would hold his hand and run, kiss him and mess with his body like a young teenager, building his dreams with one flower next to another, while he grew with her. 'Now she wants to demolish them all!'

'Nooooo!' A wounded wolf howled inside him, the whip of rumbling time pattered in his heart. He said 'no' a thousand times and he would continue to repeat it. 'She will stay with me!' Death danced in his chest, confused hope rushed in his head. 'I will tell her everything today, I will surprise her by what I say. I will get angry, I will yell and wring my wounds with her. I didn't destroy my life except for her; she will not be able to slip away from my hand, under any excuse whatsoever.'

The street was dark; some cats were messing around in its shadows. He threw a look towards the entrance of the building and stopped, stunned. There, in the shadows of the dimly lit entrance, two ghostly figures were entwined and oblivious. His mouth fell open; his throat became as dry as the desert. It was her! He slipped silently into the shadows, so he could observe her without being seen. Brutal blood roared in his temples. Everything about her indicated a delicious surrender to the lips of the man she was with. He was older than her, quite tall and thin. He had a bushy mustache, intensely white under the beam of scarce light. His gray hair glowed, well combed as if it had been rubbed with oil. He stopped to contemplate her eyes; he appeared a dignified man, with features more like a thinker, than a lover stalking a woman to her house.

He got closer, trying to listen to their conversation but he was surprised to hear that soft French language that he no longer heard, since Julia ceased teaching it to him, many years ago. Only their eyes and those mysterious smiles were getting inside him, like the barb of a fiery lance.

His ears began to buzz and the lights of the nearby streets disappeared. Darkness seemed to overwhelm him; the two ghosts faded and the heavy scent of jasmine coming from a nearby garden patio, that normally permeated the air with its fragrance, seemed to vanish. Feeling confined, he fled into the shadows and dark of the buried streets. Death alone can be his companion; his heart felt crushed, his eyes whiplashing the faces of passers by.

'Sordid is the name of your mother, you atheist!'[14] Horror screamed in the vault of his chest.

He roamed like a refugee in empty places, then landed in front of her door. He put his finger on the bell without leaving it. He pressed with everything he had, with all that disappointment and madness supplied him. Still, there was no one in the house. He knocked on the wooden door with his hand, he cried out loud with a crushed, puny voice:

"Georgette .. Georgette ..!"

Emptiness came to swallow his calls. He returned to the mocking streets, plowing his way through the people, oblivious to their presence. He found himself in front of a bar, one that catered for the lost and lonely, the losers in society. Tonight he was such a loser and he made his way into the bar:

"A bottle of whiskey and a pack of cigarettes."

He sat in a secluded corner, waiting for his soul to coalesce. No sooner had he finished his drink than he rushed to the phone. He called Rola, asking her to come immediately. She didn't say anything. Within half an hour she was there, silently caressing him.

"Do I look stupid to you?"

"Never!"

"Naive?"

"What is it with you tonight? Why do you say these things?"

"I want to know."

She pressed his hand in sadness, without answering. She realized that something was tormenting him.

He gazed at the big mirror in front of him, he saw himself as a giant ghost with the eyes of a wolf and the body of a lion. He compared his muscular arms to the arms of the owner of the bar, the arms of the waiters; he defeated everyone. He looked to his right; one of the customers was sitting alone, smoking his cigarette and smiling to unseen things that he perceived in front of him. Every now and then, he would curse the occasional remnants of the drink that clung to the tip of his bushy mustache. He was a large man, his big belly falling down to hit the table in front of him.

"Do you not see how this impudent man is making fun of me?" He suddenly said, with the muscles of his face rigid.

"Who?"

"That man." He said, indicating to him with his eyes, which were now filled with blatant anger.

"I don't think so; he seems busy with his drink and perhaps, dreaming of things that concern him."

"No, he is gazing at me, mockingly. Did you not see his sarcastic smile?"

"Calm down Selim, please!"

"He thinks I am naive, weak and could easily be devoured." He said, getting up angrily.

She grabbed his arm to try to dissuade him from it but he pulled his arm violently and went to him:

"Do you think yourself a man?! Come, show me your manliness."

The man lifted his head, flabbergasted as he looked at the young man who stood in front of him. Suddenly, Selim's eyes fired with anger and he waved his fist in front of the man's face.

"Excuse me sir, I did not understand what you said?" The man responded, somewhat calmly.

"You have to understand a lot of things. You think I am easy to devour, don't you? Now stand up and apologize, or else!"

"Or else what? Are you crazy, man?"

"Crazy! I will teach you who is crazy!" Selim yelled, as he hurled a heavy punch at the man, who dodged it while trying to hurl a reciprocating punch but a crowd of able-bodied men had managed to separate them. Still, the man who was attacked managed to land a punch, piercing through the arms of the restrainers and bloodying Selim's face.

He felt the taste of warm blood wet his lips, which made

him lose all remaining sense. He began desperately flailing, trying to reach the man but the others were able to prevent it. They hustled him to a remote table, trying to calm him down.

He rested a little while, then his head felt heavy, his body gaunt and tired. So, he left the place quietly, as he heeded the calming words of the owner of the bar. Suddenly, he remembered Rola and turned back, searching for her but she had vanished. He asked the bar owner, who told him that she went out a short while before, after paying the account. His eyes returned to the street, the bustling lights and revelers filled his vision. He pushed himself through a group of young men who were circled around a lit billboard; he passed through them impulsively, blindly, without paying attention to their angry words. He crossed the road and entered the quiet side streets that were scarcely lit.

Slowly, he began to calm down. However, his wound began to throb and he raised his hand to examine his split lip. He felt the warm viscosity of his blood on his fingers. He stopped in front of a pale street lamp, wiped his hand and lip with a small tissue he got out of his pocket. Then, he continued towards the main street, lit with its colorful lights scattered across the many billboards. He felt the glances of revelers stinging his body and his face. So, he quickly crossed the street, not caring about a car that swerved in front of him. The driver tried hard to avoid hitting him as he yelled curses and shook his fist.

When he found himself in front of the entrance to his apartment, he was seared by the smell of urine. It shocked his senses and his dry nostrils trembled. His eyes extended toward the dark corners and he crossed the entrance quickly, avoiding looking at the place where he'd seen the two ghosts. Still, his ears strained to pick up her voice and his head clamored with the resonance of an old bell.

He stopped in front of the door out of breath. He then threw the palm of his hand at the bell and pressed non-stop. He heard her steps approaching, rapid and agitated. Poisonous blood flowed to his face. No sooner had she opened the door for him, than he pushed it with his hand and entered, squeezing himself between her and the door.

She gasped, bewildered as she looked at his bulging eyes and his swollen lips, where a thick thread of blood had clotted and extended to his chin.

"My God! What happened to you?" She said in a terrified voice, as she pulled him towards the big sofa. She sat near him, inspecting his lip and the bruises on his face.

"Did you have a fight with some one? How wicked of you! ... Ah, you are drunk; I will make you a cup of coffee."

He lifted his head, which was bent on his chest and said with an old voice that came from deep within:

"We will get married! ..."

Her silence and her blank eyes answered him, so he repeated while holding onto her hand:

"We will get married! ..."

"I will make you coffee." She repeated as she suddenly rose, while trying to free her hand.

"Do not prevaricate, there is no longer a way out. We will get married tomorrow, I will never leave you."

She felt his warm breath on her hand that he raised to his mouth.

"Hey, calm down a little Selim! You are tired and sick. I will get you coffee and bandage your wound."

"No, do not kill me! I want to end this farce; we have to go back to our earlier relationship. We will get married and leave here. I can no longer stand this place and I feel I'm in a trap. I love you Julia but he does not, he does not! ... " His voice came out intermittently and his breathing was frantic and fast.

"We are going back to what we were like in the past and I will never go back to her. You are the one I love. We shall live happily together. We will dance naked on the beach. I will do whatever you would like. Only you and I, do you hear?!!"

"All right, all right, calm down a little. Let me wipe that blood."

She entered the kitchen momentarily, returning with a bottle of disinfectant and some tissue. She started to clean his lip and his chin quietly, while his hand caressed her neck, touching her ear.

"We will get married, will we not?" He said as he caressed her chin.

"Calm down Selim, let me finish cleaning up your chin. There is thick blood clotted on it."

"Hey, you will not leave me Julia, say it!"

She threw the tissues in the glass ashtray without answering.

"Say it Julia, please! ..."

"You are exhausted and you have to sleep now. We will talk in the morning, go to bed."

He caught her shoulders while that groveling sparkle glowed in his eyes, then he whispered:

"We will sleep together."

There was something in his face that made her back up, to try to escape from his hands, saying:

"No, you are delirious."

"I am not delirious, I love you, Julia. You know that." He crushed her lips with his mouth, then started to kiss her neck, while holding her strongly:

"We will get married, right?" He said as he looked into her eyes, relaxing his hands.

"Why do you have to always torment me, you know this thing is not possible, stop it please!"

She rose up angrily and rushed towards her room, as she felt his hands slipping away from her body. However, she could not close the door for he was faster than her. He put his foot between the door and its frame, then pushed forcefully and entered the room. He held her strongly and started to kiss her, ravishing her neck, his hands like two panic-stricken birds pulsing strongly over her lean body, his body a stiff trunk that crushed her soft flesh. She screams at his face, begging him:

"Let me go, please!"

He covers her lips again and she feels the taste of blood wetting them. His wound has started to bleed, blood dripping hotly on his chin and staining her lips and face.

"You are bleeding; you have stained me with blood."

He did not hear her words; his head was pervaded with the scent of lust, his eyes seeking the past, flowing through a blemished horizon. He pulled her towards the bed, so she started to resist his strong hard hands. He threw her onto the bed, falling on top of her.

In a moment everything had changed. Blood fled from her face and warmth vanished, leaving her body as cold as ice. Her eyes were suddenly blurred with transparent thin clouds and their light was extinguished. He felt the cold leaping to his body, shards of ice piercing his trembling fingers on her neck. He gazed at her challenging, vacant eyes. He was stung by the contempt of silence and that smile, stained with his blood.

He extended his thick fingers around her neck, touched her throat, then pressed with his thumb; he stretched his palms around the neck and started to press. His heart thumps in his chest and he presses, his eyes fade in his head and he presses. Singing birds flee, the few dreams are defeated, her face is getting more and more yellow and her breathing is intermittent under his trembling lips. Two heavy tears fall and collide with the tip of her nose and then proceed slowly down to her lips. He saw those iced clouds cracking in her eyes and that beam, which suddenly glowed, then faded behind her eyelids, which she violently clamped down.

He loosened his hands, pushing his head into her chest. When he felt her hand playing with his hair, the cold fell back and was replaced by this warm tranquility. His hands searched for and enclosed her other hand, then little by little he slipped into a deep sleep.

* * *

12

How his eyes bulged as he approached him. The poor man was drinking, while contemplating mysterious things and then he would suddenly smile at an idea that occurred to him. However, when Selim approached him yelling, his preoccupation faded, stumbling over his chair as he stood, stunned to see Selim's angry face. Maybe, what frightened him the most were those prominent teeth under his upper lip. They often scared me when he stared at me with those mysterious eyes, as he held me with his great arms.

When he called me at that late hour, we had not been parted for very long. We had spent a nice day, although it had started cloudy with his quarrelsome questions but the sea brought him back to his serene temperament. I now know, that the sea makes him as happy as a child; he drowns his eyes in its depths, contemplating its waters, deeply fascinated until it looks like he sees its deep secrets. I always choose the sea for a place to meet him; he speaks without raising his eyes from its blue rippling surface, except to look into my face suddenly, so I feel that his eyes are moist from the ocean rippling in them. Coldness slaps me, so my eyes freeze on his eyes, then he goes back to release me from my captivity and plunge into the sea again.

Something about him makes you feel like you are sailing in a sea of impossibilities. My relationship with him in the beginning was nothing but a simple amusement, for I often feel exasperated by these dreamy personalities. They speak to you about the soul and things that are not seen, like they are living in another world. I loved to irritate him all the time; he seemed to me to be goofy, spending his day waiting for Julia. He has remained a stranger to the city, despite the long years he has spent here. He has no acquaintances except Julia's acquaintances; he has no desire but Julia's desire.

"What a dull cat he is!" I told Julia one day, as we were crossing a street after I'd visited with her for some time. "How do you live with this guy, doesn't he seem tedious to you?"

"He is kind-hearted, not as you think."

"But his looks are naive and idiotic, as if he is learning everything for the first time."

"It may seem so but there is something noble inside him."

Drop by drop, his amazement and mystery started to increase my desire to know him but he had remained stubborn, like a flint stone. Julia's relationship with him amazed me; they have always seemed to me like they were formed from different clays and then there is the age difference. I wanted to know what Julia admired about him and may be more, what he liked about Julia. I stumbled a lot over his impetuous, fast answers; he was getting more mysterious the closer I got to him. Yet, Julia was encouraging me to go deeper with him.

In the beginning she was alluding to the establishment of an innocent friendship, to save him from his deadly loneliness and help him to enter the city lights. However, with each step, I would feel her pushing me into his embrace. I did not resist, something in his eyes began to pull me to his arms; a desire to dive deep into his innermost self. So, I began to dive but he remained like a bottomless sea. I dove deeper and deeper, yet I always found myself on the surface, swimming slowly. Julia knows this. She is the one who always tells me the dates of her absence but without indicating that she knows. She would just call me, saying:

"My dear, I will be absent for three days, please tell Georgette so."

Of course she could have told Georgette herself but she wants to tell me: 'Go to him, I have left him alone.'

I know this woman well; she always gets what she wants. She has become bored with him, this poor guy and now she is with someone else to abate her boredom. I met her when I moved to a new high school. She was the French language teacher there and I had to pass the baccalaureate exam. I sat in class, listening to her giving French language lessons in a correct accent, explaining French literature as if she had lived with this writer, or that. The muscles of her face shrinking in grief, when the hero suffers longing for his sweetheart and her face lights when he escapes from a trouble that had befell him. She narrates, representing his personality, laughing with his laughter and despairing with his misery. In the classroom she was always serious, she did not allow us to get out of the subject. Yet, when we go out to the open air, we would have fun with her like a young friend. She really looked much younger than she was, playing, dallying around, dancing, having fun with us as her companions. She became the focus of all our admiration, we sought her company with an indescribable desire but she was always choosing whom to befriend and I was one of those. She would say:

"I admire you Rola for your great vitality; no doubt we will be friends."

When I invited her to a small party at our house last year, she came with an old man who looked past sixty, despite his serene rosy face but the wrinkles under his eyes showed his age. He was dignified with his white hair and an elegance that reflected his youthful spirit. As for her, she seemed to be crazy about him; she remained stuck to him throughout the night. Even when she impressed us by that wonderful dance that she performed, amid everyone's admiration, she continued with her eyes glued to his eyes, as if to say: 'this is all for you.' They looked like fantastic lovers. Even at their age, there was something that makes you feel the joyful spirit of teenagers, who were dallying with their liberated flesh.

I have encountered him a few times since; I used to pry on him with my questions, taking advantage of her absence. He was quiet, moved slowly and he answered my questions with a smile, without losing his patience with me. His words come out as if from a deep well; warm, seeping smoothly into the depths of my spirit, so I would feel reassurance and warmth in his presence. When Julia would come back, she would join us like a butterfly that had just emerged from the cocoon, wings flailing in excitement and would say in lively cheer:

"This little devil has caught you, no one escapes from her hands."

He smiles at her words, replying:

"She is a wonderful bird and needs someone to tweet to."

Did Selim know about this? No one can say for sure; his silent eyes warn you of the consequences of the answers. When I asked Julia about it, she said slowly while escaping far away:

"He knows everything and he does not want to know anything."

I often tried to lure him but he always answered with alert neutrality, leaving me a great expanse of doubt.

His attitude seemed strange that day; there must be something that torments him. He is very attached to her; he does not seem to live except when he is near her. Even I do not seem to him more than something de trop. I could not win his heart for he is still attached to another world, eating all his dreams. 'Do I really love him?' I have often asked myself this question and the answer has always come shaded with the unknown. Something makes me rush to him without thinking, waiting for an opportunity to be alone with him. I feel a baffled cautiousness when his gaze falls on my body and my heart falls into a deep well when his eyes cling to my own. Even when such an overwhelming desire to irritate him sweeps through me, his eyes sailing into the far distance defeat me. No sooner had he called me, saying: 'I want to see you,' than I answered him in the affirmative, even without asking him why; I did not even think of my answer that preceded me, saying: 'I will come immediately.'

I went out speedily, I sat near him holding his hand and I realized he needed me. He was sad and bleak; talking about things that seemed to me difficult and very ambiguous. Suddenly, his facial expressions changed and his lips began to tremble as he looked at himself in the big mirror. Then, he attacked that poor man who defended himself and was able to wound Selim's lip. I could not follow up the fight; I left the bar after they separated them and took him to a remote corner, trying to calm him down.

The street was lit, filled with loiterers. I walked a short while and then I went back to the bar, my desire for him intensified; when I approached the bar, I saw him coming out with the effects of the fight clearly upon him. I rushed up to him, calling him but he was walking as if asleep; he passed by me and went on without seeming to have heard, or seen me. I went back home, feeling despair.

The next day I did not go to the Faculty of Commerce where I was studying, rather, I went to him. I knew that Julia would be at her work, while he waits until half past nine to leave, so I pressed the bell with confidence. Julia's face peered at me, while she was still rubbing her eyes and her face was strangely pale.

She did not seem amazed by my surprise visit. She invited me to enter, saying coldly:

"Please come in, I shall wash up and come back to you to drink coffee; I have stayed up late and I feel tired."

While she entered the bathroom, I began arranging an excuse so I can justify my morning visit. I started to stroll around, my eyes searching for him; I checked his room through its wide open door and I saw his bed still tidy. 'He does not seem to have slept in it last night, or perhaps he woke up early.' As for her room, it was locked. 'Maybe he did not return yesterday, oh how crazy I am! Why did I let him go alone? He was not in a condition to walk alone.'

Julia returned, carrying the coffee tray in her hand. She sat down next to me, so I took the initiative by saying:

"I came for the book; Maha has requested it, so I thought I would ask you about it."

"The Book! Ah, of course you can take it."

"You seem to be very tired; your eyes are so red. You must have stayed up late yesterday."

She paused momentarily while she gave me a glacial, harsh look, then continued:

"He has returned drunk yesterday, he seems to have been in a fight with someone; his lip was injured."

There was a suggested accusation in her voice, so I said with a bit of a challenge:

"Perhaps you are somewhat responsible for this."

"Maybe!" She said, turning her face away, then added in sad tone: "He is still asleep for he is very tired."

"Asleep!"

My eyes darted towards her closed room. 'Then he is there, he slept in her bed.' My thoughts wandered in the yards of the past; I knocked on the closed doors, then I returned back to her eyes to ask brazenly, with a deliberate smile, which I hoped would provoke her:

"But I do not see him in his room, is he in the hospital?"

"No, he is in our bed." She replied coldly, pointing to her room with her eyes. Her coldness stung me in addition to that, 'our bed,' which she said in a strange accent with a light smile on her wilting lips. It made my chest constrict with rage and intensified my desire for challenge.

"Would you like to see him?" She said, after a period of silence.

"No, not now, there is plenty of time later on." I said

smiling, looking for my words, seeking to irritate her. "But did something happen between you and Mr. Jameel[15]?"

The muscle of her left cheek shrank and her forehead crinkled a little.

"Mr. Jameel is an old friend, you know that."

"But he is handsome and single, he is more suitable for you."

"I don't think so; besides I have terminated my relationship with him."

"Why?"

"Because I discovered that I love Selim more."

"Oh, really!"

"Certainly!

"Maybe!" I said as I stood up, taking leave.

She did not move; she remained seated without accompanying me out[16]. I went out, slamming the door after me. What was happening was rather strange. 'Did this old woman finally wake up to the fact that sleeping in a room next to her, is a young man in the prime of life and stopped messing with that old man?'

For the first time I felt something eating me up from the inside. 'Is it jealousy? But I have never felt jealous before! And why today in particular? Is it because I knew that he slept in her bed?' I went out into the street conjuring angry words of defiance: 'What a driveling crone! She believes that she can regain him but for how long?'

In the following weeks, I deliberately went to him more than once on the weekends as usual but Julia was always on the lookout for me. She no longer left him; their relationship returned to its past glory and perhaps more. He seemed happy, blood flowing to his face with strange vitality. When I told him that I wanted to see him on his own, he said with some regret:

"Forget the past Rola, we're getting married soon."

"Who?"

"Julia and I."

I was shocked by the surprise, so I said angrily as I stood

ready to get out:

"She betrayed you, the bitch!"

"No need for this, Rola, you are wrong about her."

I returned home with decrepit dogs licking my face. My mother was in the kitchen and my little brother was lying on his stomach, reading his schoolbook. I passed by his room as I rushed to my own, at the far end of the long corridor. I closed the door, throwing myself on my bed. I burned with rage, so I began to sob in a subdued voice, cramming my face into my pillow. I felt an unfair defeat. 'A crone past fifty, her body stiffened and her skin soiled with those dirty wrinkles, throws me out like a dog!' I threw my pillow, looking to the big mirror with hatred.

Everything related to her turned into nasty dirt; I began to hate even my memories with her. Perhaps, I also hated myself because I smiled at her one day. I felt the weight of clothes on my body, so I took them off and lay naked on my back, looking from time to time in the mirror admiring, my voluptuous, beautiful body. My chest felt congested with a swelling poison, while thin tortuous leeches preyed on my guts. I hit my pillow with my palm and then ... I dozed.

The next day I went with my dad to his office; he owned a trading company and his office was full of staff that showed him a lot of respect. When I told him that I wanted to accompany him to the company he was very pleased; he often asked me to get to know the work, he would say:

"I do not believe in those differences they make between men and women, I believe you will be able to manage the company well."

His dream was for me to sit in his place and manage the company. This dream had seeped into me little by little, so that no sooner had I passed the baccalaureate than I joined the Faculty of Commerce. There was nothing standing in my way; since my childhood I have felt my consequence. I always got what I wanted; clothes, trips, even when I wanted to visit Europe last year, no one could stand in the face of my will. I told him that I wanted this, besides I was no longer young, he hesitated a little and then approved, in spite of my mother's insistence; she always hallucinates with unjustified fear. My father always silenced her complaints. He would say to her:

'Take Samer and leave Rola ... Don't you see how you've made him a shy coward with your permanent dread!'

My little brother Samer, who is past thirteen years old, has come to fear going down the street alone; he stays alone at home between his toys and books. He doesn't go out except when my mother wants him to and then only when accompanied by the maid. As for her, she rarely goes out with him, as her many friends don't allow her a chance to do so.

My father is a serious man, everyone admitted to his power and success. So, when we entered the company's building, heading to his office, I was not surprised to see their eyes full of admiration and respect when they greeted us.

We sat for a while in his office and he showed me the business he runs, then we went to visit the various company departments. It seemed to me that everything runs smooth and easy. I didn't find any difficulty in understanding the multiplicity of its work. Rather, I felt a sense of pride in my future position. When we finished, I decided to take a drive; this sense of pride was the lever I used to persuade my father to let me drive his luxurious, white limousine. He refused at first, saying that I could take the other car but he was forced to bow in front of my insistence. I went out to the lot where my father's car was parked. I sat in front of the steering wheel, touching the precious fur that covered it.

It was a new fur cover, which had been recently replaced; for my father is fond of new steering wheel covers. I took a small mirror from my leather purse, checking my face and my hairdo. I was pleased with my look, which I found very appropriate to the body hugging, White Cowboy ensemble that I was wearing. I took strength from my appearance. I turned the car on and took off. His office was the only place where I could find him alone. It was located on the other side of the city, so I took a complete turn until I reached the broad promenade, adjacent to the beach. I loved to drive in the places that allowed me to pilot a car at high speeds, feeling the soft sting caused by the fresh sea air. There were many slower cars in front of me; I overtook them all, enjoying the amazement of some and their looks, full of awesome admiration at seeing a girl beat them all.

When I arrived, I took a look at my clothes and my hair before I left the car, then sprang up those broad marble stairs towards his office. I stopped in front of the fat employee, separated from her by a glass barrier, saying:

"I want Mr. Selim El- Radi, please."

"Mr. Selim is not here, he has taken a long vacation." She said, while contemplating me with amazement.

"When?"

"Today."

Everything seemed shaky, the glass barrier swayed and her face twisted, becoming rectangular to the extent of hideousness. I turned around, jumping down the broad stairs. Everything looked like it was in retreat; even the houses, cars and distant ships appeared to be fleeing in panic.

My car roared away as I clung to the steering wheel and threw my weight on the gas pedal. Dust blew out, forming a whirlwind when I took to the white, dry dusty pavement, to pass by a car that lumbered in my way. Only moments had passed, then I was climbing slowly the last few steps to his apartment, trying to catch my rapid breath. I stopped in front of the door a moment, listening, then I pressed the bell button several times in succession but its echo came back, empty and bleak as if someone was playing music in a cave.

* * *

13

I woke up at noon; my head was heavy and my body felt like it was made of lead. The memories of yesterday's events, started to knock my chest with a sledgehammer. I stared at the empty part of the bed, searching for her. The door was closed and behind it, a heavy silence began to press its octopus-like tentacles around my neck. Everything is warning of a disaster, the speckled blood stains on the white cover, the scattered pieces of furniture, the smell of air heavy with humidity ... 'Will I see her again?' My eyes pleaded with the closed, wooden door. 'What did I do? Oh what a scoundrel I am! I could have continued in this manner without resorting to my foolishness, at least she is with me and has not left me, despite everything, now would she stay?' Everything says no, the closed windows, the gray shadows in the opposite corner, her torn dress thrown under the bed, all staring in despair and screaming: 'No, no!'

I got up out of bed, dragging my stinking body towards the closed door. I stood in front of it, feeling this silent horror that claws at your guts in front of the abyss. I opened the door slowly, my eyes scanning the living room. My eyes suddenly hit the wall of her silent eyes. She was sunk into the

big velvet couch opposite me; I felt something pierce my
chest like a thunderbolt. I lowered my eyes, still frozen in my
place. She got up quickly and came towards me, saying:

"You seem pale, are you okay?"

I caught her hand, without raising my eyes from my chest.
Then, I said in a hollow, hesitant voice:

"Julia ... I am sorry!"

"No need for that, you were drunk. It seems you are still
tired, let me help you."

"You don't need to trouble yourself, I'm okay."

I let go of her hand and entered the kitchen but she did
not leave me. She accompanied me to the sink and started to
help me to wash. She dried my face and my lips, removing
traces of clotted blood. From that moment on, things
changed spectacularly. She stayed beside me without leaving
home; she exercised her role as a woman, while I looked
astonished by what was happening. The color of her icy eyes
and her broken smile did not change, nor did her face take on
the dreamy expression it used to when I kissed her. Still, she
no longer left the house and she brought me back to her bed,
enjoying that volcanic warmth, so I slept deeply while
breathing the smell of her milky breasts. Although I sensed
that her wooing actions were forced with a rusty mechanism,
I was keen to forget this. Perhaps, I could have enjoyed this
as a regretful return to me but her deep inattentiveness, the
loss of her eyes into a distant aspiration, continued to scare
me. I waited for her to invite me to the seaside, as in the past
but my waiting melted into her hollow eyes. So, I took the
initiative, saying:

"How about we go to the sea this evening? Don't you
remember our old days?"

"We can go if you would like to." She said coldly, forcing
her smile.

We went to the same place; the beach was deserted as
before, its golden sand obscured by gray shadows. We ran
naked on the beach, played in the water, lay down on the

sand, contemplating the sky as in the past but everything seemed trivial and silly. It had lost its magic. It could not compete with my imagination, which for a long time had painted events with myriad colors, changing the distribution of shadows from time to time.

We returned to the house after she was worn down by fatigue and I was crushed with fear. She slept immediately, while I stayed beside her, contemplating the broken corners of her mouth, struggling with a stiff insomnia that was splashed in the dark corners of my head. As soon as I woke up in the morning, I rushed to her, repeating my old wish to marry her. She looked at me quietly, then said:

"Do you really want to do this?"

"Want to do this! I don't dream about anything but this, Julia." I said, panting over her neck. She laughed for a long time. For the first time since she returned to me, I felt that she laughed without affectation.

"Oh you naughty boy, you want to marry an old woman! Where will you come up with children?"

"It does not matter!" I said with joy, as I nibbled her ear, so she continued laughing nonstop.

Within days we were in our home[17]. We finished the marriage procedures without any hindrance worth mentioning and then we returned to Beirut, after a short stop in Baalbek. She insisted on returning for only one day, before we went back to this beautiful village, high up in the lofty mountains of Lebanon, where a friend offered us a small villa. She said she wanted to liquidate some of her business with the school administration. I stayed at home, alone all day and in the evening of the next day we were sitting in the garden of that wonderful villa. The villa was very luxurious, which made me hesitate before I lay on its elegant beds. This made Julia laugh at me, as she pushed me onto one of those beds.

We had a long summer ahead of us, to spend together. Everything seemed beautiful and fun at the time. The sky was colored with a quiet blue, wild birds sang and flew over the forests of pine and wavy fir that rose toward the sky.

We could have napped at a gurgling fresh spring, or climbed the mysterious mountain behind us; from its summit we could have seen the sun set with its charming auroral colors; under the shade of its trees we could have enjoyed the bizarre melody that was launched by thousands of birds and insects. Yet, Julia wanted to stay inside the garden of the villa. It was a really beautiful garden as she said, still, the mountain and the spring, the river and the adventurous summer birds, all of them were tempting me to explore but I deterred my desire and stayed with her.

She used to wake up early, go out to the garden where she would stay until I got up and we would eat breakfast together on the patio. When the sun began to scorch the earth, we fled to the terrace, enjoying the view of deep valleys covered with pine trees and deep oaks. At night the TV was our only entertainment, we would stay in front of it until Julia's head rested on my shoulder and I would caress her neck, saying:

"Go to bed, my hands are numb."

She would open her eyes, smiling, then get up leaning on my shoulder. I would follow her with my eyes until she closed the door after her. Minutes later I would turn off the television and hurry to her. I used to feel her waiting for me; she would open her eyes a little, then hold me and fall asleep again. I would look at her face a while, then float into a warm sleep, feeling a delicious tranquility in my chest that made my eyelids close quietly.

It was no more than two weeks after we arrived there, that I began to notice those sad vacant looks, which seemed she was unaware of her surroundings. She would sit in front of the small pond, sunk in absorbed distant contemplation. She would not leave this place except when forced by my throwing a word, or question at her. Then, she would answer briefly and quickly return to her vacuum. I decided not to leave her alone; always accompanying her, trying to amuse her with conversations that I would fabricate with difficulty, or with jokes still stuck in my memory. She would respond to my conversations and jokes with a light smile on her lips, which would settle for a few moments and then disappear from her face, which began to be stretched and pale. I told her that we could return to Beirut if the place is not suitable but she replied that it was a very convenient place and she was happy here. I tried to persuade her to a walk near the river for a while and she agreed. So, we decided to prepare what we needed to spend the next day between the trees of the near valley.

The next morning we began descending the small dirt road towards the valley but we had not gone half the way, when she felt severe fatigue. Sweat gleamed on her forehead, rolled down her face and her breathing became strained. Concerned, I returned quickly to fetch a car to convey her back to the villa. I tried to involve a doctor but she firmly refused, saying that it was simple fatigue caused by the sharp sunlight and would disappear after she rested a little. I was unconvinced but did not want to nag at her, so I yielded to her wish.

The first month went by without me feeling that there was anything indicating a significant change in her condition. Maybe some wilting in her eyes, her cheeks and wrinkles that began to appear clearly under her eyes. I woke up one day to find her sitting on a small chair, staring into the void without leaving her cigarette, which was moving back and forth to her mouth rapidly. I jumped out of bed, calling her:

"Julia, Julia, is something wrong with you?"

She looked at me like someone waking up from a deep sleep, saying:

"No, nothing. I could not sleep and I sat to soothe myself. Go back to sleep don't worry."

The next week I had to bring the doctor, against her wish, after she was hit by excruciating pain in her guts. The doctor said it was an ordinary spasm and advised her to take care of her food, after prescribing her some soothing medicine.

Her health continued to deteriorate, her face seemed pale and she continued to lose weight.

"What has happened to you, Julia?" I said, panicking as I observed her loose dress slip off her shoulder.

"I don't know, I feel tired, I will try to pay attention to my food."

Yet, over the following days, my fear increased when I heard her panting as she ascended the steps up the small stairs. I called the doctor immediately, he advised us to conduct general tests, before starting treatment. The next day we were boarding a taxi, heading to Beirut. I contacted Georgette in Beirut. Georgette took care of everything quickly; she led her to a large hospital, accompanied by her brother, a doctor, who worked at the same hospital. Everything was fast and the next day we met the old doctor who supervised her examination. He said with a smile:

"The lady only suffers some intestinal disorder. She has to pay attention to her food, as well as stopping smoking. It is hurting her lungs so much."

Shortly before our return, he bent to my ears, saying:

"Take good care of your wife."

I looked at him in wonder, but he had moved away, still smiling to us from afar.

Julia remained the same without getting better but I got used to this situation and no longer felt afraid. I started following the doctor's advice. As soon as I came back from work, I would sit near her, trying to entertain her with flirtation and long talks about desultory things, deliberately staying away from the past and its memories. Yet, when I tried to convince her to go out, she smilingly apologized, referring to her inconvenient health status.

There was no longer anyone visiting us except Georgette and her brother, the doctor, who continued to come with Georgette from time to time, to check on her.

In the early days of our return, many friends appeared, especially her colleagues at the school where she worked, as well as many of her students who clamored around her. However, after the school year began, friends dwindled until they finally disappeared.

Julia had stopped working at my insistence, until she recovered her health.

Everything seemed ordinary and routine; I woke up in the morning to go to my work after we ate breakfast together. I came back at four in the afternoon to find her waiting for me, we'd eat lunch and then I'd lie down for a short siesta, then I'd return to sit with her.

Things had become covered with gloomy shadows and our talks began to dwindle to short words, amid spiraling smoke circles in front of her, while she plastered her hollow eyes on the living room wall. That was until I woke up one night to find her sitting alone in front of the mirror, opening her little white box. I began to observe her face reflected in the mirror, while she bent to that box, which was full of the treasures of her secrets.

Her eyes were gleaming through tears that started to slowly descend to her flat lips. She raised her eyes to the mirror and I closed my eyes to slits, so I could see her without her being aware that I am awake. She took up her cosmetics and began to paint her face, which seemed less pale after she wiped her eyes with a tissue.

When she was done and started making her charming smile, I could not resist the sight of her new image, which fully opened my eyes in surprise. A charming face with sparkling eyes and cheeks lightly flushed, I jumped out of bed yelling:

"I swear you're the most beautiful woman in the world!"

She suddenly rose up with her face constricted, her eyes extinguished and then she said, with some reproof:

"You have startled me, I thought you were asleep!"

"How can I sleep with your charming eyes sparkling over my head?"

I approached her, trying to kiss her but she suddenly noticed her box, so she quickly closed it while standing up to face me, smiling. Everything in her was shaking, her delicate feet, her white breasts that descended slightly and her lips, which had returned to their ripeness. I carried her in my arms, while kissing her face.

Things began to light up as in the past, when angels flapped their magical wings. I thanked God, worshiped her eyes again. I thought this fatalistic butterfly would always live in my soul.

The world had really changed a week before her departure, suddenly she was turned into a transparent dove, which made me spiral madly about her charming spectrum. We went out to the alleys and crowded streets. We carried the night with its wandering dreams, under our arms. We wore madness, worshiped at the feet of insanity and then we ran to the sea, to the beach, deserted except for us, to sand startled by our footsteps. We dallied like two drowning souls in its joyful waters and then we ran naked, as we panted after the laughter that escaped from us.

"I adore you!" I whispered, as I sprinkled the sand over her naked breasts.

She looked at me through a lock of hair that scattered over her eyes and then jumped silently towards the sea. She knelt down in the shallow waters, looking to the distant horizon and then she seemed to pray, silently. I called to her frivolously and she did not answer, she remained looking far away. The dim light of the moon bathed on the surface of her face. I waited a moment, then went to her. I brought her up from her shoulders, gently and then we went back to the beach together, while I held my arm protectively around her bare shoulders. She looked at me and whispered:

"Forgive me!"

The waves were clashing in her eyes and a golden beam shone on her face, she kissed me longingly, while squeezing my neck. After which, we lay on the sand observing the sky that had taken on a strange bluishness. We stayed on the beach until late and then we went back to the house, after we grew weary with fatigue and hunger. As soon as I finished dinner I resorted to bed, feeling very sleepy but she remained awake.

I woke up at night and didn't find her next to me but I was too tired, so I continued to sleep until the morning. She woke me up unusually early. The signs of fatigue were visible in her eyes, in spite of her skill in the use of cosmetics. I did not want to ask her about it; in recent days I avoided indicating the symptoms of her illness. She had prepared coffee, so we drank it together while she talked to me. She spoke about things that seemed to me, mysterious and filled with exotic worlds, while she searched with her eyes for invisible things. She talked about life, about the sea, about the countryside, about the enchantment of the sun as it fell to swim in the sea. Then she recalled the memories of that old movie and its two heroes who were running naked on a sandy beach, as the sun began to sink into the distant horizon; she remembered those auroral colors reflected on their bodies while they were laughing. There was an enchanting sparkle in her eyes and it touched my soul with a cool, delicious tingling. So, I remained glued to her eyes, baffled by those words coming from her lips, like someone who speaks from afar. She caught my hands, looking into my eyes as I was getting ready to go out and then she kissed me, while holding my face with her palms ablaze with glowing fire. She accompanied me to the door, saying goodbye but suddenly returned and pressed a kiss on my face, saying in whisper:

"Goodbye."

I jumped down the stairs to the street; every part of my body was saying 'Come on, come on, hurry! You have to return early, finish your work quickly and come back, she is waiting for you, her heart, her body, her eyes and even her delicate lips are calling to you.' So, I came back early, I came back quickly, skipping to her and she was waiting for me, but ...!

* * *

14

He entered a flower shop, bought a small red bouquet, then planted his face in it, devouring their scent as he left. He stopped on the sidewalk, contemplating the empty street. The cold wind stole into his neck and then withdrew, along with his eyes, to trees of the small garden, which fell amid the branching road network.

The yellow leaves were falling slowly, whispering among the dense branches, only to flutter a bit before landing atop of their companions with a sleepy murmur. He felt a distraught quiver as he listened to the sound of the street sweeper breaking them under his feet. Thus, he fled with his eyes to the sea, through the only portal that ran through the crowded buildings. He realized that it would not be long before the gap was closed with another towering building that may hide even the white clouds behind it.

The sea seemed noisy and rough, slapping the sharp rocks with its waves, as if trying to escape but to no avail. Just as soon as it breached some of their jagged spires, it would slip down back again, exhausted. His dreamy visions were broken, so his eyes dropped back to his black shoes, stained with patches of mud, only to climb slowly to his red bouquet, to smell it again and begin to ascend the long street.

It had been forty days since she died but there was nothing to make him think about commemorating her 40th day memory, according to traditions[18]. He only had a few acquaintances, so he preferred to go to visit her grave alone. It gave him some comfort to sit near her, to talk to her even though she could not hear him. Near her, warmth spread and the air floated full of intoxicating, dreamy scents.

He entered the cemetery, passing through its black iron gate. He lowered his eyes as he walked between the crowded white tombs. He was afraid of seeing that majestic white vault, above which hung a picture of a young girl framed in black. Her wide, black eyes extended their gaze towards him and he would feel the tremor of death arresting his chest, then seeping into his back in a cold stream. He crossed by quickly, trotting toward Julia's little tomb at the eastern end of the graveyard. The cemetery was empty, except for small birds jumping suddenly from one place to another, seemingly unafraid of anyone.

He felt a slight shiver when he turned to her small marble grave, that ominous tombstone declaring that she lies here. He traversed the distance that separated them, slowing his steps, which began to plod above the stiff soil under his feet. Caution crept slowly up his long legs as he gently knelt on the chest of marble, kissing the picture of her face and then tucking the small bouquet of flowers exactly at her nose. He lingered a while, resting the right side of his face on the marble surface, like someone who listens to the deep and delicate whispers of those passed. He was not interested in that lizard which had stopped in front of his face for a moment, twisting its sharp tongue like a Turkish dagger dancing in the hands of a clever knight. Nor did those bulging eyes alarm him, diving into the depths of his eyes, defiantly. Only it's tense tail with fast quivers made him close his eyes against the treacherous sword of dreams. 'I did my best. No way was it ever my fault,' he muttered, suddenly hunching over himself as a deep cry reverberated in his head, echoing over and over:

"... Seleeeeem ... , Seleeeeem ...!"

He caught his head in his hands, squeezing his ears as he tried to keep that desperate scream away. He seemed unable to escape from the eyes of that fatalistic lizard and its shaky tail behind it.

"Do not go today, Selim, for the weather threatens of a storm."

"No, I have been absent yesterday and it seems to me that the weather will be good today."

"But, Selim, the river ...!"

His aunt stopped kneading the dough with her lean hands, she began trying to remove its sticky remnants from them with traces of fear showing in her eyes.

"The river will rise my darling; you will not be able to return."

"I can return via the gully."

"The gully! Are you crazy? It's so deep!"

Her facial features tightened whilst she removed the black veil on her hair, which was liberally sprinkled with gray.

"You have nothing to fear, for we are used to jumping over it easily."

She gazed into his face, observing those rebelling eyes and a pale smile came on her lips, causing his chest to quiver.

"Do you remember Selim? I was like you, not afraid of anything until someone came and explained to me that I was nothing compared to Him."

"Who?"

"Who! ... I don't know but I know His ominous, almighty ability. Pay attention to yourself, Selim. Don't be deceived by the strength that you feel."

"Don't worry, I will not commit a foolishness. We will go together, Ramez and me."

As soon as the last lesson ended, they jumped out and began descending the slope toward the village. They were aware of the hardship of this dirt road, sloping down to the river. The rains that fell so profusely yesterday had dampened the soil, transforming it into slippery mud that was hard to walk on, especially at those rocky cliffs. The rocks became dangerous when streaked with mud and perhaps, even more so with the green algae that spread over them. They were well aware of this through the many times they were forced to cross those narrow paths. Caution is necessary in those moments when death lies at every curve. Still, how could they be cautious when the wind was blowing violently, whipping their faces and necks with repeated blows that pushed them towards the slope?

"I wanted to see her today, if it were not for your rush!"

Ramez looked at him with reproach, while holding on to a protruding rock with his hand, trying to resist the wind, which was roaring strongly. His long blond hair and green sparkling eyes, like those of a sly wolf.

"How can this be my fault? If we had not returned quickly we would have had to stay there, for the storm is coming! Can't you see?" Selim replied angrily, feeling Ramez's characteristic sarcasm in his admonishment.

Although their friendship went back to childhood, there were a lot of differences in their disposition, which made a lot of people wonder about the secret that brought these two extremes together. While Selim was shy and more often than not, introverted, Ramez was a young liberated adventurer, often rude, insolent and storing inside his head endless obscene phrases, which he discharged with the same ease he ate pastries. A lot of his colleagues feared him for his strength and his insolent tongue but he remained the focus of everyone's admiration for his intelligence.

Selim hated his domineering, braggart temperament. He often scolded him over those foul words that he uttered before the girls. Selim used to dissolve in shame when Ramez started some bawdy flirtation and he listened to those answers fired by girls, which were no less lewd. Yet Ramez, despite all that, was the focus of attention by many beauties;

who may have complained of his lewd dalliance but without losing their permanent smiles, or their coy laughter.

Yes, he envied him. He wished in his secret heart a thousand times to get rid of his cowardice, to allow his lips and tongue freedom, to go ahead and flirt with them using the same lewd words, the same lecherous signals and gestures. Still, paralysis remained on the alert, creeping into his hands and tongue numbly when one of the girls attracted him with a movement of the hand, or a blink of an eye, or a smile. When one of them fired a suggestive, out of the ordinary joke, or when sarcastic lewd flirtatious phrases began to be showered upon him, that damned blurry cloak smothered him. It's fug clinging to his temples and covering his chest heavily, so he retreated into himself, fleeing to the sanctuary of nearby corners and looking for Ramez.

Ramez looked up at him one day with a smile, he said:

"Don't you see man? Only look in front of you; she keeps staring at you."

"Who?"

"Hey! Don't try to bluff me, lover boy! Look to the left and right and you will see her. Only wink at her with your eyes and you will see her between your hands."

"Saud?"

"Of course, you fox."

"Do you really think so?"

"Of course, move a little and you will find paradise in front of you."

He loved her. He was swept with thick clouds when she passed in front of him. The blood flowing in his face rebelled on him when she smiled, or threw her laughter in his face. She was sitting in the seat directly in front of him. So, he was able to observe those heavenly black eyes when she bent over to her colleague, or that pink mouth kissing her pen with enchanting transparency and sometimes that marble neck sparkling under her long black hair, cascading onto her back and shoulders.

'Does she love me?' A lilac bird throbbed in his chest and his blood ran cold when she looked at him with those eyes, wrapped in ancient mystery.

'Does she love me?' In his head, he turned over every sound or whisper, every word or signal and concluded with that fearful answer, '... Yes! ... '

"Talk to her! At least give her a sign. Do you think she will come to you begging and saying, 'my darling I love you, have compassion for me.'?"

"Enough glibness! ..."

"Well, I will take care of this task."

"No!" He said, angrily turning with his eyes toward the nearby woods.

"Then get in touch with her, write her a message. I can write it for you if you want me to, I have words that can tame the most beautiful woman. Don't be afraid, it is a tried remedy."

"No! I will write to her myself."

He ripped up many pages before he resorted to a book, which he remembered contained messages for lovers. He selected a passage that he considered was the best he could write, then ended the letter with several love verses, which he found in a magazine. Then, he pressed it into Ramez's hands, who took it happily.

He waited most of that day. He stood under the big maple waiting for Ramez's return. The wings of fear pulsated in his chest; love hummed avidly in his eyes and danced in his pupils. His infatuated lips were waiting, his numb legs rapidly paced the narrow dirt path back and forth and his tense nose, with its frozen beet red tip, pointed towards the distance. Even his thick index finger had not escaped; it had taken to touching his thumb with worried, fidgety strikes. 'What will she say?' The question tormented his mind endlessly and mad Ramez was very late, or so it has seemed to him, for time was transformed into small circles overlapping each other endlessly. He ground his teeth in anger. 'Is he deliberately late to tease me? The bastard! Does he believe that by doing so he's better than me?' Angry ideas clamored in his head, turning into threats and challenges. The red anger of a captive taken by force jammed into his eyes, so his hands contracted into fists and he almost screamed. He was about to return home when he saw Ramez. He walked with bowed stature; playing with a tender twig he had smashed parts of.

The air suddenly grew lax and the world became a bubble of silence around him. Challenging swords evaporated from his eyes and he asked, with some impatience:

"What happened?"

"She refused."

"She refused to receive the letter?"

"No, she read it and then handed it back with the threat that if you repeated it again, she will tell whom it may concern."

The bubble of silence burst, nature returned as mistress of the situation. The morning birds whisked by with their wings outstretched, searching for their food; dirt snakes writhed, hissing between small bushes scattered here and there. Insects croaked and buzzed in all parts of the forest. He, alone, was devoid of life amid this overwhelming vitality.

"Don't bother yourself. She is nothing but a stupid boasting woman, there are many others." Ramez offered, trying to find an excuse for his friend's failure but it was impossible, for failure is a castle with impregnable towers. It could not be defeated; not even by that girl who convinced him to go out with her in one enchanting moonlit night, nor by the one who fell upon him with her mature body in search of a lover. She, this arrogant witch with her heavenly black eyes, remained the only one to blow the breath of life into nature.

"It seems to me that the gully is the only place we can cross." Ramez commented, looking defiantly in Selim's eyes.

"So be it, a big leap and we are on the other side."

The place was no stranger to them; they often crossed the river at the gully, with a wide leap they knew well. In the summer the river water became scarce; so the river was transformed into small creeks running here and there until they converged at this narrow point. Here, two huge stone slabs lay, with a spacious passage beneath them where the water ran. In the winter, while torrential deluges rumble, coming from distant mountains, the river was seemingly confined in a narrow area, no more than a meter and a half wide. However, inside this fallacy was hidden a rough thundering torrent, running between those innocent white flagstones.

Although he couldn't remember anyone ever having fallen into this place, few men dared to take this adventure. Indeed, the expert eye would be aware of the huge danger that anyone would experience if they did fall in when the river rebels in the winter storms.

Selim slid on the sticky mud and fell as he tried to catch up with Ramez, who had bypassed him by a short distance.

"Were you hurt?" Ramez shouted, startled when he heard the sound of his collision with the muddy ground.

"It's nothing." He replied as he stood, brushing the mud stains clinging to his trousers.

"Come on, hurry! We must reach it before the rain."

"And how can we speed up in such a place? Don't you see how the earth has become like soap?"

Ramez waited until he reached him, then they began to walk together.

Once they arrived at the river, they stopped for a little while at patch of short green grass and started to rub the bottoms of their shoes free of the mud stuck to them. When they were sure of the cleanliness of the shoes, they started to walk on the big white flagstone near the water.

"Jump first, Selim and I will follow you directly."

Selim looked at the strait, which was filled with water almost up to the edge. The water was clear and calm, no signs of its flow showing on its surface but the deep growl was forewarning the size of the adventure. Selim retreated a few steps, then went skipping forward and leapt. His foot was able to pick up the slab and then the other foot settled firmly on the solid flagstone on the opposite bank. He continued jogging a few more steps, trying to verify that he had moved sufficiently away from that treacherous gap. A smile of triumph rushed to his lips as he turned to meet Ramez with a face glowing with strength and joy, when he heard that deep thundering cry, as his friend fell between the jaws of the gully.

" Seleeeee ... m!" He cried, then disappeared for a few moments. Then his head came up a little, as he resisted, beating with his hands at that wide mouth which was pulling him down. His pleading, bulging eyes pursued Selim as he screamed, his letters stalled as the water swallowed some of them:

"... Seleeeeem ..., Seleeeeem ...!" Then he disappeared again.

Selim rushed to try to save him; he lay on the flagstone immediately, hanging on to a slippery rocky lump, clutching it with one of his hands and extending the other hand toward the water and cried, declaring:

"Ramez ... Raaamez ... Grab my hand, grab my hand, Ramez!"

But his call was in vain; his hand waved above the water searching fruitlessly, then plunged into the water in search for Ramez. The deep waters of the river had swallowed him, pulled him down into it's depths and did not leave him until it had absorbed his young spirit. Then, it ejected him far away where the men of the village found him, having jumped up, panicking when they saw Selim screaming from afar and running towards the village.

He remained near him on the day they heaped the wet dirt over him. He wept near him; he clung to the rocks of his grave like a madman, until they carried him to his house after he had been defeated by a fever. He remained, struggling with that terrible fever for days. It clung to his body sarcastically, mocking his eyes as they hid in an unjust horror. In his bed, he kept replaying those terrible moments; that pleading scream and that head hanging between water and air, those bulging eyes that had desperately beseeched him. 'Could he have done anything? How could he justify this to his sister, who kept screaming at his face whilst they heaped dirt on his body, her hair flying in all directions and her face torn with crazy scratches?'

"You left him, Selim! You left him! You criminal! Would he have left you if you were in his place? Coward! You will remain a coward, you traitor!"

'Yet how? Could he have jumped in after him? Then they would have died together. He did his best.' He'd exposed himself to the same fate when he laid on the slippery rock, trying to pull him out but the river was faster than he was. It seized and departed with him. If he had been able to catch him, he could only have fallen with him. In his torment he wished for it so much, burning flames flared up in his chest. 'Take me to the river, throw me to it ... I want water ... I want water, we must die together!' The cold water would come up to his forehead, then he would sense this warm hand putting compresses of cold water and gently caressing his face as the other hand holds on to his.

'Seleeeeem ... Seleeeee ...!' The cry built up in intensity, becoming aggressively thunderous in his ears. He looked for the lizard but he did not find it. It had left the place and disappeared into one of the many dens that plagued the cemetery.

He kissed the marble and turned around to return. He wanted to get away as soon as possible. He passed through the gate, turning his face into those cold breezes that blew from the west to bite his neck. He took a deep breath, smoothing his hair. He lit a cigarette and took a long draft of it, then walked across the street.

He was walking, probing the asphalt street with his feet; trying to verify that the street was solid enough to bear his body filled to overflowing with heavy, confused guilt.

He stopped under a small tree, contemplating the sea, which he glimpsed through the high-rise buildings. He lit another cigarette after he threw the first, which he had sucked up until the burning filter stung him. He looked at his watch and found that only half an hour was left before his appointment. Rola had told him that he would meet him in the café for reasons that concerned him. Yet, what would really matter to him after this? Death, which stole from him the remnants of freedom, had driven him to fall into a deep bottomless pit, which he didn't know how to get out of. Georgette, Rola, Jameel, his boring work and the desolation twisting like a snake between the walls of his house; all were consuming him without mercy.

Rola didn't wait for long; she descended upon him at the moment he least expected. She literally came on the day of the burial; she disconcerted him with those lupine looks, as she threw her arms around his neck. She embraced with sadness, saying:

"I am sad for you. I never forgot you, even though that door had been closed in my face."

He looked into her eyes as he gently pushed her away from him, without saying anything. His eyes were two piles of burning coals and his ears were empty vessels after Julia's last whispers. She left when he wanted to stay, he who was reclining behind departing time, crying out for her, kissed by hot tears spattered on his lips to be sucked by that salty taste of his stiff spirit. But Rola, that glass girl, did not leave him alone; she defeats him in the den, locking his eyes imploringly. She came by every day, she would not leave his home until he fled to the nearby street, lurking among its human globs of meat and turning to those false sands, desertified in fear of water. He lays down on it, fleeing from it and to it, then reclines, sinking down with his dreams as his pillow ...

Julia comes in her transparent white robe; she comes floating above the air, hovering around him, smiling compassionately. Yellow and sad with the corners of her mouth turned green, whispering from afar: 'Forgive me, I have loved you.' He whispers to her, extending his hands, 'Forgive me, I have worshipped you.' He approaches her, trying to pick up her hands outstretched to him but she suddenly slips away and melts in the wind. His fingers thrust into the dry sand, squeezing a handful, as he rises up heading towards the sea and screaming:

"Mirage .. mirage .. Even you are a mirage!"

He returned to his home for her to hold him in her beseeching arms, robbing him of his missing eyes. She kisses him and he retreats in panic as he sees Julia's waxy face dropping between her lips:

"Forgive me, I cannot, I feel sullied! ..."

"I know, I am trying to help you forget." Rola whispered with a sad face and forced smile.

"Leave me now, please!"

"Alright ..... but tomorrow we will go to the sea."

"The sea! No, I don't want to see the sea."

"Alright then, the mountain."

Thus, he goes with her like a secret that was missed by two people, like blood that was spilled over nothing. He surrendered to her hand, so she caught his hand, squeezing the rest of the blood and he panted in search of air. She kissed him at every oblivious crossroads, so he naps away behind her eyes and her fluttering hair that whispered on his face: 'I will never forget you!' His eyes scream as they search for Julia in the ether but in the evening he falls asleep upon her breasts, that glass girl, that doll girl.

'Was blood pumped into her body? Had the sea breezes crept into her breath?'

Suddenly, the glass was stained with the deluge of blood branched out into its folds, those eyes trembled with the bustling colors of life and safe warmth seeped from under her arm pits.

'Oh, is it possible?' A dark question idled futilely in his head: 'Is it possible?' The question returned to noisily knock in his ears as he got out of the taxi and stepped towards the sidewalk. He lunged with his eyes towards the café adjacent to the sea, searching for him behind the glass windows that framed the circular building. He was sitting near the window overlooking the sea and had turned slightly, so that he could see the street without being deprived form the pleasure of looking at the sea. He greeted him with his hand as he stood up, ready to receive him:

"Welcome Selim, please sit down."

"Thank you."

He looked at his face, observing its freedom from the wrinkles those of his age are supposed to have. His blue eyes seemed wrapped in the veil of the unknown, sailing non-stop in the floating glare of his clear eyes.

"This is perhaps the second time we meet?"

"I cannot recall a first meeting." He said somewhat drily.

"Ah, you are still angry! I have really acted in a reckless manner, I let my passion lead me; it was an adventure, was it not?"

"Maybe." Selim muttered, pelting him with acerbated, incendiary stares. He was assaulted with memories of that fateful day; when this old, white haired man with a bent head came into where Julia was lying on her bed peacefully, amid women wrapped in scared aghast sadness, looking at their own inevitable fate. He stormed the place silently; even his breath was dissipated in the space of the room, in lax stillness over her waxy body. He broke into the human wall like someone walking in a bubble, without seeing anything, his dark eyes sailing in an infinite space of sadness. A castle of emptiness, which suddenly faded when he fell on her body, curling his body up at her feet as a baby; he kissed those wooden feet with the holiness of a mad man who had just escaped from a nearby asylum. When he approached her face and pressed his wet lips on her bluish mouth, his eyes washing her face with his abundant hot tears, one of them muttered in humility:

"Oh God, how great you are!"

As for Selim, he was paralyzed by surprise; he was

astounded by the presence of that man whom he immediately knew. Suddenly, he was assaulted by his deeply buried pains, all his desires for murder and revenge. The trembling fever of death rushed to his head, ravaging his dry eyes. He could have broken his scarlet neck when his lips sullied Julia's mouth, he could have folded him over himself, breaking his bones and then throwing him like a rag into the middle of the street when he stopped a moment in his place, looking at Selim with fatherly love...... but he did not lift a finger. He remained frozen in place, even his tongue became lax, to the extent that it seemed he would never utter another word.

He was assaulted by the memories of that treacherous storm and his rebelling courage came back to him. He clenched his fist strongly in front of him, murmuring: 'Ah, if only he had stayed for another minute!' It seemed to him that the surprise and speed with which he'd entered and exited, were an acceptable justification; any man would have been thunderstruck and paralyzed by surprise, when a man enters with that audacious insolence and does what he did.

Today, however, the blood did not climb to the temples, nor did his hands clench, just a bit of dry sadness leaked into him as he went back to that memory:

"I could have killed you at that time; you have acted in a manner I could not forgive. If I had not kept my head, you would not have liked what would have happened to you."

"And now what do you think?"

"About what?"

"With regard to that incident, do you still want to kill me?"

"No, it's over and done with."

"Do you hate me?"

"This was when there was a reason to require it."

"And now?"

"I don't know, maybe something of those unpleasant memories."

"Did you see me as a competitor?"

"Competitor!" He exclaimed, throwing angry stares at him; those defiant words that put them together on the same level, annihilated him. "Never! Never did I consider you a rival, maybe you seemed like a thief!"

"A thief!"

"Certainly; you wanted to seduce her, did you think that in doing so you would have been praised?"

"But, couldn't there have been something other than this?"

"Everything is possible except for love. Maybe you are rich and this is what shows on your features and clothes, you could offer something that I don't have. I always felt Julia's desire to enjoy life but I could not offer a lot to that end, otherwise how do you explain to me a relationship with an old man like you?"

"But Julia was not young, besides she was much older than you. So, can you explain to me how she would marry a young man so much her junior?"

"We were in love! Besides, what business is it of yours! You have invited me for some reason that I don't know yet." He retorted testily, trying to get rid of this annoying subject.

"Do not get angry, my friend. I don't want to annoy you but perhaps this conversation is linked to what I want to say."

"Then I can leave, I don't want this!" He rose up with the intention of walking away, then he heard that velvet, quiet sentence ......

"And what if I bring you something from Julia?"

"Julia!"

"Yeah."

Selim looked silently at his quiet face and his wonderful eyes, then gently sat down as his frown eased.

A period of silence ensued, broken by the waiter coming to put two glasses and two bottles of beer on the table. He then turned back, after taking leave of them with a sober smile, which remained stuck to his lips until he had gone several steps away from them. Selim noted that exotic icon that hung on his chest by an antique silver chain and that bronze ring with its emerald, atop his polished ring finger; he seemed old and venerable, sailing with his eyes silently on the ocean waves.

"Do you like the sea?" The old man asked, without looking away from the ocean.

"Maybe, I love and fear it."

"Well, at least we seem to agree on loving it. In a time gone by, I used to love the sea. I felt it was merciful, hiding in its unknown an enchantment. I was on the other bank, extending my eyes to the horizon, dreaming of those magical worlds that float on this beach. History was always in my pouch along with my dreams until ..."

He stopped for a moment, his eyes returning to Selim, who had remained silent as he listened to his words ...

"Until I was defeated ..." He paused again as memories washed over him and drifted away.

"Are you a stranger to Beirut? In fact, I have guessed it; your accent indicates that. Maybe from Aleppo, is it not so, Mr. Jameel?"

"Jameel!" He repeated the name, returning back to the sea with his eyes, floating on its surface, immersed in sad reflection. He then turned to him, saying in a hesitant absentminded voice, like someone talking to himself:

"I have really almost forgotten my name ... almost forgotten my identity, my language and my mother's tales in our old house."

"Have you left Aleppo a long time ago?" Selim asked, affected by his sad eyes, which were clad in a misty twilight.

"Ah! ..." He smiled with an abstracted sadness, which remained in his eyes and then he continued, after a brief pause in which he refilled his glass:

"I left its prison bars a few years ago."

"Its prison bars!"

"Yes, my friend, I was a prisoner there."

"What did you do?"

"I killed a man."

"Why?"

"A fight for the girl."

"The murdered man must have been a competitor?"

"Not at all, he was her uncle."

He paused for a moment, and then said, staring into Selim's eyes:

"Do you know, Selim who that girl was?"

Those sympathetic expressions faded from Selim's eyes to be replaced by a growing bulge of curiosity, which froze in search of the answer.

"She was, my friend, that the young girl called Julia."

"Julia!"

The dunes of gray sky landed on him, piles of stormy bitter cold thundered in his eyes, tremendous masts tumbled, rumbling on the chest of a sinking ship.

"Yes, my friend, Julia ... Julia, that beautiful wonderful girl. That woman hidden behind the forgotten destiny, in her fenced grave. Her last wish was for me to tell you, to tell you what she had lacked the strength to tell you."

* * *

15

I could have strolled by the sea shore along with Jan, or resorted to one of the large casinos scattered on this beach but something deluged in darkness, drives me to stay. What is this tarriance to which I am driven? Alone, held between terrified panic-stricken walls of desolation and great silence. Silence croons deep down inside me, a trembling fear aiming at escape, yet I remain fragmented behind closed doors, waiting for salvation.

I feel impossibly dizzy with bustling futility, looking for nothing. In the vacuum of loneliness, I refuse futilely, slightly nauseous; I don't know why my head is floating today around memories of distant past, moaning in my chest and obliging me to stay in bed. It is not illness at all, rather her quiet reassuring voice, as she tried to convince me to go back on my decision.

"... God has given you a chance to survive, He gave you a chance to take shelter in Jesus' mercy, do not allow the devil to overcome your spirit and contaminate your soul. I am talking to you, sister Georgette, because I have had the same experience before you. Satan attacked me with all the temptations of this world. He tried to steal my soul by embellishing life and placing its pleasures before me. But a sister older than me in this convent, was able to expel him with her pure spirit of faith in the tender mercies of the Savior. I realized that what I was looking for was nothing but a pretty transient life, Jesus was always with me, shading me with his tender bright Spirit, warming my soul with his quiet smile as he is crucified on his cross.

Sister Georgette, go and pray, take shelter with Him; ask for His mercy and He will always be with you. Jesus who was tortured for the sake of our salvation, who was crucified on his cross for the redemption of our soul, will not leave you ... Go, sister Georgette, and kneel at his feet, ask for the salvation of your soul."

The air was trembling under the cover of soft white clouds; her voice was flowing deep into my spirit, transferring to me the remains of my fugitive soul. I felt His spirit touching my head and slipping into my chest like a gentle cool breeze, the dim golden beam seeping into my eyes with delicious warmth.

"I will go, sister, I will go. I will pray for the salvation of all our souls." I said, tears welling, trapped in my eyes and then I fled to him. I remained kneeling in front of his feet, praying, as I resisted Samir's eyes that racked my spirit, pleadingly.

I'd met him at our house, on one of the visits that I paid to see my invalid father who was strongly besieged by disease, which had incapacitated him and thrown him in his bed, in search of his close salvation. God was close to him. He would pray to Him, his eyes rushing towards his wooden cross, which hung in front of him murmuring, trembling, delirious. My father had always been a religious man; he made God seep into our souls through the blood he bequeathed us and then through the word of God, which invaded our hearts eagerly, searching for salvation. Perhaps, my mother was less influential than my father; God was, for her, only a slogan and rituals she performed without thinking about them. She accompanied my father to the church; she repeated the words of the Bible that she had memorized, she knelt humbly in front of the statue of the crucified Christ. Still, she would go back to her daily life without faltering in the words and proverbs of the Bible, which stuck to my father's lips. My mother had died a few days after I entered the convent. She had tried to stop me with all she had, tears welling in her eyes, in the face of my father who encouraged me to do this:

"My daughter, we have lived throughout our lives as believers, fearing God and not committing any of the sins He declared forbidden ... Why do you have to bury your life at such a young age? You can save your soul without this."

I was seventeen when I vowed myself to God, following the example of Saints whose extraordinary biographies touched my dreams so that I wanted to become like them; wrapped in that warm holy halo as I tried to spread the word of God on earth, in search of the salvation of human souls, whose sin has brought them to this permanent torment.

I eagerly embarked upon the study of theology and the Bible, which drove me to pursue philosophy in my university studies. I got used to my new attire; I can even say that I felt myself turn into a Saint, whose spirit floats about this tormented world. I often saw myself wandering around places where life was pitiless and hunger domineered. I would move among its weary and fatigued people, conveying to them the word of God and His tidings of another, happier life. I would see myself sharing with them that dry bread, as their eyes were sparkling with the joy of a great hope.

Christ was always with me, accompanying me even on those few evenings when I was alone, recalling my innocent childhood, which was filled with surprise at all that I saw and that beautiful life in my teens, which filled my head with a desire for a carefree life.

I finished my university studies still absorbed in that austere life, mocking outside life and its modes. The words of God floating over the letters of my books and ideas, conveying to me that tranquil dream of the salvation of the world and its rise to His kingdom. My soul hovered at the banks of His enlightenment, basking in that eternal carefree happiness.

Until I was sent to that school which follows our sect, God was only a transparent and luminous entity, overlooking us with His tolerant, bright, merciful face. It seemed to me that all the philosophical and religious phrases that described him as Almighty, were nothing more than absolute good, absolute love. Until that big, heavy car fell and shattered Nagy's body, that little boy who was no more than ten years old. He was a blond, beautiful child, overcome with shyness and introversion when I saw him for the first time, sitting alone in the garden on one of the seats, nibbling a small piece of candy. I didn't know what attracted me to those green eyes, watching the other children as they played on the green grass. I approached him and started to speak with him, he seemed to me gentle and sensitive, his words tender and transparent, carrying all that innocence with which the angels of heaven were crammed. God filled his spirit, his soul embracing the one crucified over his cross, praying at his feet, telling him about his childish, innocent aspirations, brimful of good will for all.

When the bereavement occurred, I had become attached to him. I felt that his pure, innocent soul increased my hopes for a world empty of hatred, filled with love and the desire of absolute good will. He was sitting alone in his usual place, sending his eyes out to the distant void, his innocent smile filling his angelic face with the brightness of a permanent dream. Suddenly, that big car fell and started to tumble over the cliff that separated the road from the wall of the school. It broke the fence and then fell on him, crushing his tender body. Only his head remained alive for a few moments. I was among the first who rushed to him; the trunk of the car had settled on top of his body. I approached him, while others tried to push the car from his body. His face was yellow, while his eyes were burning with a strange dream. I put my hand on his head, crying:

"Nagy, my darling!"

He swallowed his saliva with a bit of difficulty and muttered:

"I love you so much, I have prayed for you yesterday."

"My darling!" I screamed as tears sprang from my eyes, mean and perfidious, while I saw his eyes close and his lips trembling. Then his cheeks shrinking and everything was turned off.

I looked up to the sky, begging and angry; God had taken the color of those black gloomy clouds, His eyes angry and malevolent, wearing His military regimentals, threatening with his mighty sword, blood trickling from its shiny blade. However, when one of the naughty students asked me days after the accident about the secret that makes God takes the lives of innocent, good people, I answered without hesitation:

"It is God's will. He takes these tender angelic spirits to spare them the experience and keep them pure in the bliss of His paradises."

However, God was no longer that White elder, who radiates pure light. My heart was stained with the bright red blood that flowed from Nagy's body. I have started to turn to Him in fear and terror of His almighty killing sword. I have become afraid of His angry, malevolent eyes as they looked through the dark black clouds. Only Jesus, that spirit dedicated to our salvation, remained wrapped in that pure light, with his pale face, which radiates pure love and good. He became my refuge when I fear God, I kneel in front of his feet, complaining:

"O Savior, you who prayed and were tortured for our salvation, save us, spread the shades of your mercy on our souls. We have received our lives, not through us, or our efforts and assiduity but through your mercy and through your Will, you will save our souls to your eternal light!"

When I am shocked by the bustling, exhausting life, I resort to my books in search of something to calm my troubled soul but God was getting paler and angrier, his eyes wrapped in that cruel hatred, eager for a lot of blood. 'But why?' I screamed inside, scared and panicked.

"Have mercy on me, Oh God, have mercy on me for I am brimming with sin, save my soul from the jaws of the devil!" I scream, kissing his wax feet, which were penetrated with an iron nail, so blood radiated out of its wound. However, I kept wandering between panic and mercy, not daring to disclose my secret to anyone.

When I met him in our old home, he welcomed me with a smidgen of extra respect that demonstrated contempt. I felt his reluctant, dry gazes fall on that black coarse robe that wraps my body.

He was sitting with my older and only brother, with whom he was engaged in a sharp debate about a demonstration they wanted to attend. My brother, the recently graduated doctor, was driven by revolutionary ideas away from God and perhaps he had become an atheist, without saying that. I was sitting listening attentively to their conversation, which was filled with those harsh threatening words and that glowing enthusiasm that fled in outrage from my brother's worried eyes. However, Samir kept his face and eyes neutral, in spite of those phrases eager for violence. A modicum of quiet confidence enveloped his voice and his distinct abilities to put forth his ideas, made my brother succumb to his point of view, which seemed more powerful and persuasive.

He was speaking while stealing looks at my face and his eyes were hunting my eyes, with a strong, confident beam.

I don't know how I felt that hot air creep deep inside me, as he talked about things that seemed as if they were meant only for me. He had talked about God and Christ, about good and evil. He said that God seems to be of a cruel, military bent in the Bible, while Christ came with a peaceful invocation, supporting his opinion with a lot of citations that I knew but I'd never looked at them this way. His words seemed to me to carry a lot of cruelty and cynicism; he made me enter into a long discussion about God and Christ, good and evil, as well as abstracts with him. I summoned all my knowledge of philosophy, I felt that my battle with him as a battle between God and Satan; God, who lives in my heart and the Devil, who stole him. I wanted to defeat Satan with all the power of the word of God but the word of God seemed poor and overstuffed with the unknown, before the Devil's clear powerful word.

I went back to the convent that day with the steam of defeat rising to my head. Everything in his eyes had made me feel his contempt; his defiant, piercing looks, penetrated my body wrapped in dark black. I felt the wild quiver of the flesh, so I fled to him, the one suffering alone. I knelt over his feet in contrition, but Samir's eyes remain stuck to my body, jabbing it with that primitive appeal.

I met him again the next week in our house, when my brother was forced to hurry to the hospital after an urgent call, so we stayed alone. I don't know why I felt fear and happiness; something brutish drove me to stay with him, despite my many chores. He did not raise the past discourse that day. Rather, he talked about life, about humans, about his dream of justice and happiness. In a quiet manner, he criticized monasticism and the captivity of human nature, behind the walls of a savage and cruel life. I did not feel in his smile that contempt which previously hurt me, nor in his eyes that cynical challenge, pricking me deep down.

Conversely, there was an enchanting beam in his eyes and a warm sparkle in his smile, which seeped into my chest, dreamy and delightful.

He said he was pleased to meet me, despite the fact that our views of life were different but this should not prevent our meeting continuously. I agreed with him on that point, feeling a desperate urge to save the soul of this young man who had fallen into the traps of Satan.

I began to meet him regularly; I would feel him close, warming my soul that had become frozen behind the icy banks of the dream of the eternal salvation of humanity. The convent became a prison wrapped in black, grinding my body and my soul between its harsh millstones. The moment I would leave it, I would feel my spirit cheer up, bouncing in joy at meeting Samir; that quiet young man with his confident smile, which appears through his blond mustache and his piercing blue eyes over his round, full of life, face. I would contemplate him as he moved to shake my hand, bowing his long stature and I would feel that warm glow seep eagerly, deep into my body; but the black robe was an impregnable barrier, so his eyes retreated falteringly and his face took on that light blush that affects whoever commits a sin. We were both aware that we craved to meet each other with the same strength and desire; our gazes stumble in a vacuum as we search for a discourse to fill our time, after we exhausted all we possessed of arguments to prove our points of view. Yet, the meeting remained a ritual we performed, driven to it by something hazy and brutish. I would drown in his eyes, in search of a secret hiding away in their depths, while he sits opposite me mired in a vacuum, dreaming of disclosing the secret. Then, he stopped one day as he looked into the vacuum and said with some sadness:

"I know I am not saying anything that our eyes have not said but I will say what our tongues were unable to say, until today. We have to admit that we want something beyond this relationship which is void of any explanation; we are, deep down inside, looking for the human solution. I realize all too well that a thick wall stands between us; it is that dress that you are wearing. You have to decide between the robe and love. I am proposing marriage to you. That is what I can say, enough playing behind walls of fear."

I often feared that moment, especially when he would stop with his eyes burning and floating in a vacuum. I would have indicated to him that I am not looking for a relationship beyond what is happening, if he had given the slightest signal of it. Yet, for him to confront me in such a clear and direct manner, this is not what I expected. Surprise held my tongue, or perhaps it was fear, for his words carried something strong and roaring, putting me between two choices, between two miseries. I didn't know how to answer him and what to answer, my heart escaped him in fear and my body became a burning cinder, that could only be quenched by his lips.

"There is no need to give me your answer right now; you can take your time." He added, after he saw my eyes silently flee to the distant sky.

On that night I kept tossing in bed until the morning. I could feel that painful, panicky shuddering in my body and in my head, that violent conflict. I seek refuge with Christ ... I kneel and pray in front of him, yet he is replaced by Samir's face, pushing him strongly to hang himself on the wooden cross in his place. I go back to my bed, scared and panicked; I close my eyes, so that conflict starts between the faces of Christ and Samir. I would feel his body slipping in my bed, glued to my body, so I jerk as if stung by the suffering in Christ's eyes, which pierce my head like an arrow of flame.

Tears sprang thickly from my eyes, as I stood in front of the statue of Christ weeping in pain but he remained frozen wax, his eyes fleeing to the silent vacuum. I scream at him in complaint:

"Deliver me, Oh Jesus! Save my soul from this torment. Get me out of this land to your kingdom, I am suffering and I resort to you. Save me!"

I escaped to philosophy, to seek a refuge to support God. However, it turned against me, sailing in a world of distress, swimming in a space of bewilderment. I turned to my brother, who remained silent, as he viewed that dialogue, on his lips smiles attesting to God's defeat. However, his eyes have remained petrified and despairing. I resorted to the Virgin, I prayed before her image, complaining to her of my sufferings and my torture but she didn't do any more than her son did. She remained, smiling at her young son without seeing me. I stood in the middle of the convent yard, looking to the vast sky and saying:

"Lord, I am tormented, I resort to you, help me!"

The sky remained black and terrifying, I was assaulted by

Nagy's picture as he lay in a pool of blood, so I cried out, saying:

"Why, Lord, do You take the pure and innocents and leave villains to wreak havoc on earth? Help me, Lord."

However, the sky grew darker and black angry clouds proliferated.

"O Lord, forgive me for I am a sinner!"

I retired to the convent hermitage in search of an answer, an indication from Jesus of Nazareth to direct me to my fate but they all disappeared, like a mirage does when the sun sinks behind the distant horizon. Only Samir stayed by my side, with his confident smile and his eyes shining with sincerity and nobility, his warm voice as he talks about love, hope, happiness and the good of all.

The tortured Christ started to turn into a living being, flowing into my soul through Samir's deep warm words. Did not the Bible say: 'In the beginning was the word;' and here is his word flowing through Samir's lips, alive and strong, launching the good tidings of a happy world.

"I will leave the convent and catch up with life; I feel that my place is there and I can no longer continue." I told the convent's Mother Superior, who tried to convince me with all her experience and expertise, to remain. She talked to me about Jesus and his crucifixion, about his torment for the salvation of humanity. She reminded me of the words of the Bible and the work of his apostles. When she felt she was sailing in a rough rebelling sea, she asked me to pray and turn to Christ again. I carried out her wish; I knelt in front of him, I prayed for forgiveness but his eyes remained hard and lifeless; a piece of yellow wax worn out through the years.

The next day I was running towards him, sensing an awareness of being naked within the kind of joyful, soft clothes that had not touched my body for the last seven years. Everything seemed new and delightful; crowds swarmed the streets, flowing in the sea of happy life. The sky assumed that azure blue color, while those gloomy black clouds fled. That shining smile I used to see in my childhood, returned to the faces of people. My body was not mine, merely a pile of feathers adrift in the sea of happiness, my breasts were bouncing, pulsing, rushing in front of me like two white doves eager for liberty ... freedom ... freedom ... freedom ...

I scream with him in Beirut streets among the crowds of demonstrators, my voice roaring deep and agitating in the spacious spaces, my eyes are shining with the hope of near salvation, happiness and justice for all.

My body burns up between his arms with a passion for the impossible, for the dreamy quiver, for staying secretly behind the doors of truth. Waves drive me to the other bank where life is taking place, brimming with the noisy desire of a new dream. The sun is ripe and delicious, the gentle air is drunk between our lips and we sip the smile, which bloomed in our eyes. Our hearts pump strongly with the chant of hope, flowing far away, immersed in that golden aura which wraps our quivering dream in the corridors of our pulsing bosoms.

I would look at his eyes, shining with determination and my chest would flow with that fresh joyful air. Hope would pulse for him lightly and sweetly between my ribs. God returned to His tender robe and Christ's eyes trembled with the joy of a new promise. God's words flowed in a new guise, assumed that golden bright glow and blood flowed in a torrent, permeating its rosy, dreamy body. The words of the living Christ penetrated deep down inside me, ecstatic with that tremulous sparkle flowing from the eyes of the poor of the earth, who rose loudly as they listened to my words promising a happy future.

Samir became the twentieth century Christ, his voice thundering with the hope of near salvation and the assembled masses roaring around him, hurtling behind him like a roaring flood. Eyes radiating with the joy of the dream, the voice of hope promising victory, liberation, unity and freedom.

Crowds ripple in front of his porch, demanding the fulfillment of the promise. Happy with the good tidings, which twitched on his lips and flew in their hearts like a quivering current, pulsing rapidly. Suddenly his words tremble and his eyes flee, becoming extinct behind the distant clouds as he fell dead, his blood flowing heavily through the porch. His blood splattered on the alarmed human mass that started jostling, scared as they heard the sound of rapid, torrential pistol shots penetrating his body.

The dream fell quickly; the dream was broken to smithereens, bright stars faded behind the black clouds, treacherous and cynical, destroying ripe, vibrant flowers beneath them. I fell wounded on my bed, wrapped in my bewildered defeat, hugging drunkenly the remnants of my body. I run away to the empty desolate streets, reeling drunkenly through their curves, my hands resting on the air, while his eyes glow strongly, then become extinct like a nihilist mirage. His smile settles down for a moment and then withers, panicked as his lips are distorted and strangely twisted.

I collect my scattered self and go on, stumbling over the wreckage of the past, from one street to another, from one bar to the other. The Lord was too far away; Jesus was defeated and aghast, two cynical tears dancing on his lips. Corruption fills things with the smell of places and the wilted spirit, oblivious under the silence of the truth. I flee towards it, that fatalistic corruption, I drown in it, a noisy gel scattered all over the place, scoffing at all times. I love a strong merciful God; I swim between its waves and an intoxicating unaware magic spell. Then, I fall again from one bank to the other. I don't know if God was very close, or very far away.

*   *   *

16

"Yes, my friend, it was funny to find out where I was born and why? Or, rather it was funny for me to exist in a certain place. I always felt myself sailing through nowhere; time alone was the master of fixed and metamorphic things. My soul departs with it from one wind to another, from one mirage to another. I depart, through the paths of oblivion, in search for the remains of the years behind those distant sands. Yet still, they remain, despite all this, far ... far away. They slip from between my fingers and sink into the abyss of deep magic.

The East was nostalgically engraved in my heart, a love for an unknown whose echoes vibrate from afar; clapping of swords and neighing of horses, enchanted kingdoms and palaces buried in the sand, flooded by the golden dress of the sun. Since my childhood, my eyes have been departing towards the other bank; I would stand on Toulon beach and watch the white sailing boats fade into the distant horizon. I grew on that beach, while her eyes floated behind those dreamy white boats on the other bank.

Yes ... yes ... You have asked me about my identity, about my birth. I will not laugh, I will not cry but I will say, as my father said to the captain who brought him back to France after his leg was amputated: 'I was born on the other bank, in that country, which they call France.'

Since I realized that I am a being who can hear, I had responded to my mom calling me: 'Roger ... Roger ...,' Also, the teacher added to my first name, the surname Roland. I am now called Roger Roland. However, years later, my name has grown longer after they added the title of Professor in front of it. I have become a professor of ancient oriental languages. Well and after that, there was a trip to the East, along with an archaeological mission with a thirsty need for the other bank. The ghosts of the past chase each other in front of me like an eternal insanity. I am drunk on the approaching deep silence as I touch, with my eyes, those ruins fleeing toward the city of Palmyra. A feeling of awe and stillness surrounds the archaeological monuments. Rapid images of that Queen draped in the sun, assault me as we get through the colonnaded porch. All that is left of ancient, past images permeate my head and drown in its bottomless, inner most thoughts. Zenobia, the Desert Queen, puts her hand on her son's arm as she looks down from a balcony in her palace, sending off her army with the call of victory. Thousands of bayonets rise in salutation, while swarthy, harsh faces scream:

'... Zenobia ... Zenobia! We will erase the shame of the desert ... We will water the desert sands with the blood of our enemies!'

Zenobia smiles, saluting with her hand, then bends with dignity over her son and kisses his face, so loud excited voices are raised:

'Long live Zenobia! ... Long live Zenobia! ... '

You may see this as funny nonsense, or a mad man's raving. Yet, my friend, you should never mock a dreamer, dreams most often exceed the reality. To dream is the secret of life; you would never feel the beauty of poems, nor their pleasure without the dream, you would never feel the beauty of a woman without the dream dress that wraps your sweetheart, when longing attacks you. This was Zenobia from one year to another, from one generation to another, changing her dress to a new guise; it is nothing but the transparent dream dress. Even the tang of dew and fragrance of autumnal desert were passed with her, from one dress to another throughout the ages.

I was searching for her among the defeated ruins, behind the ruined walls and inside teetering statues above the ancient soil. I was sure that I would find her, I was sure that my destiny was to be defeated in her hands, for Zenobia has not died, Zenobia is renewed every year. She blooms with the arrival of spring and she is waiting for me with her sparkling eyes, with her challenging silence, with a victory smile on her delicate lips. Her fresh spirit has pursued me since ancient times, since the Spirit of God was fluttering upon the water. I was waiting for her arrival silently, for long months I have been watching the sun sinking down every evening. Zenobia will not come, except shrouded in the sun, her eyes bright under the mysterious glare of its magical rays.

Zenobia came after a long wait; she came wearing this strong face and those sparkling eyes, showing outrage and challenge. She stood in front of me and screamed suddenly, like someone surprised by a predacious monster and then, in an angry tone, she said something I did not understand.

I jerked up quickly, trying to understand what she was saying but I was not able to do so. I had not learned Arabic yet, so I said in French:

'I am sorry, I am a foreigner.'

'Foreigner!' She said in astonished French.

'Yes ma'am, I am French.'

Her angry appearance suddenly changed and she fell into a long laugh as she said in French:

'Ha, ha, ha, ha ... colonialism is back again, oh to the glory of France!'

I shouted angrily:

'No ma'am! I came for the glory of love, for the glory of Zenobia!'

'Zenobia's glory! Oh you are crazy, are your mad glories not enough for you?'

I don't know what made me enter that large orchard, which was located at one of the borders of Old Aleppo. I often passed by it as I drove my car out of Aleppo to the spacious plains but I was never tempted to enter it before. Yet, on that day I had felt a strong desire to lie down under its trees.

'You speak French very well, were you in France?'

'Never, I have learned in school and from my uncle's French wife.'

Zenobia looked out of her defiant eyes while the wind blew lightly, slipping on her face and her hair, making tender that tempestuous, fiery glow in her cheeks.

My eyes rebel slightly as they fell down her ripe body hidden under her long green dress, then I return to her face quickly, fearing the loss of her eyes. I ask her smilingly:

'Do you hate France?'

She gazes at me harshly, then her eyes move away as a hesitant gleam tampered with them:

'No, I hate cruelty and war.'

'So do I, for my father lost his leg in this land.'

'He was in Syria?'

'Yeah.'

'And you came looking for your father's leg?'

'Maybe ... maybe ma'am.' I replied, staring into her eyes and with my voice faltering in my throat. I knew I was diving deep into my fate. Zenobia stands in front of me in a moment of fear and eternal tremble, so I flow towards her, a broken voice defeated by the years.

'Is this orchard yours?'

'Yes, it is my uncle's.'

'Your uncle! So you are on a short visit?'

'No, I live in his house.'

'Do you not have a father?'

'No, he was gone since I was five years old, the French killed him.'

'Why?'

'He was in the mountains.'

'And your mother?'

'She departed with her new husband a few years after his death.'

She stared into my eyes for a long moment, then turned around as if to leave, so I jerked back to reality, calling her:

'Zenobia!'

'Zenobia! Ah, no, my name is Julia; don't you like my name?'

'I am sorry! Your name is beautiful; I don't know what made me imagine that your name is Zenobia. It seemed to me that you look like her.'

'I look like her! And how can you know that? Were you ever with her?' She said, laughing as she fluttered her hands in front of her chest.

'Perhaps ... perhaps, Julia. I have always felt that I was with her, going along with her from one era to another, through the silence of years.'

'You are very romantic.'

'How about you?'

'I don't know, I can only say that I am like this.' She answered laughingly, extending her hands to their limits and fluttering like a bird.

'Like this?' I said, smiling, as I imitated her movements.

'Yes, like this. Something that can only be described as such.'

'Don't they have some name for it?'

'Maybe, but I don't know it.'

'Well .... but how can I know it?'

'Easily.'

'How?'

'Extend your arms to their limits like me, all right: Now close your eyes tight ... start moving your hands like the wings of a bird, great ... and now continue ... continue 'til I tell you it is enough ... ha, ha, ha ... ha, ha, ha ... '

I opened my eyes quickly as I heard her floating away laughter. She had stopped a few steps away and she said, amid her mischievous mirth:

'And now you can fly ... ha, ha, ha ...'

Then she turned around and began running, fleeing away, so I called to her:

'Zenobia! ... Zenobia! ...'

She stopped, turning towards me, her face overflowing with joy and saying:

'Yes, Monsieur Uthaina.'

'???'

'As long as I am Zenobia then you must have a name.'

'No, my name is Roger, Roger Roland.'

'I am Julia.'

'Ah, Julia ... Julia Domna.'

'Ha, ha, ha ... oh you are crazy! Where do you get these names from? I am Julia ... Julia ... ha, ha, ha ...' She said laughingly, as she disappeared behind the fruit trees.

'Julia ... Julia ... I will return tomorrow, I will be back tomorrow and I want to know.'

'Go back to your country, you crazy man, you will not know anything.'

'No, I will be back ... I will be back ....' I screamed at the top of my voice, as I watched her departing path through the orchard by the vibrations of the branches as she passed by."

* * *

17

Selim had been reading these withered yellow papers for a while, his eyes glowing violently and his face burning with a simmering flame. He throws one of the papers and continues:

"... I do not know why his eyes were always dreamy, nor do I know the reasons that used to throw him far away and all of a sudden. He would rise up abruptly as if stung, loosen his hand out of my hand and then lie down, leaning against the trunk of an apricot tree, his eyes fleeing away towards the sky. I felt his swift breaths, while his chest beat violently as he pursued the clouds scattered above him. He would stay in this condition for a moment, then slowly his eyelids began to blink closed in fast movements, his lips trembled as he turned back to me with his eyes covered by a faint glow. He would bend to me swiftly and start to kiss me with a strange, childlike covetousness, his breath rippling quickly over my nose. So, I would press his head between my hands and hug him strongly.

I loved him to the point of madness; I felt his spirit storming inside me as an eternal secret, a fear clothed with the love of madness. This hidden insanity drives me to him like death, lying in wait to claw my body since birth. He was the trip of my birth and my death, my eternal search for love, for a great passion. Madness departs with us from one silence to another, from one fear to another; we embrace our tree and drown in an eternal dream. I sit waiting for him behind the branches of pistachio trees, I observe him from afar, as he crosses the fence and walks slowly towards our ancient tree. He looks right and left, then lies on the green grass. He takes his cigarette and lights it quietly, then starts sending its circles of smoke while fleeing away with his eyes to the sky.

A mischievous streak flowed inside me like a devilish spirit, so I would await him to lean on his elbow and surrender to a long dream. I put my hands on his shoulders strongly and I shout at him with a coarse voice in Arabic, a language he does not understand. So, he would jump, shaken from his reverie and turn to me, ready to fight. Yet, he would soon return to smiling, as he says in French: 'Ah, you have startled me, I thought it is your uncle with the bushy mustache.'

He was very much afraid of my uncle after I told him about the intensity of his hatred for the French and of our old traditions, which would put us in dire consequences if they saw us alone in this orchard. Fear shaded our meetings, beating in our breasts an escalating pulse at every voice, or scratch caused by the many insects and birds of the orchard. However, we would quickly go back to our childish frivolity, jumping from one place to another, undaunted by high walls that separate our eyelids.

It always seemed to me that we were two secrets, pulsing with the love of the unknown. We each came to the other in

177

search of hope, the universe scattered in front of our oblivious steps in the journey towards the impossible. I don't know why I always thought that we were running after the impossible, after a fate lurking for us like a snake waiting for a chance to betray our happiness. I could see it in his worried eyes, in his panicked silence as he took his leave of me, saying 'goodbye.' Something in his chest bustles noisily as he holds me to him in goodbye. He would hardly reach the fence when he would back up and run calling:

'Julia ... Julia!'

I caress his hair a little as he says to me in whisper:

'I love you!'

He would then kiss me violently, before he suddenly leaves me and flees, running. I knew he would not be able to cross the fence except in this way, so I would wait for him 'til he finishes his insane rite. Then I would be overwhelmed with fear, so I run in the opposite direction, crossing the long distance to the house, which was located at the other end of the grove. When I arrived I would immediately enter my room, I would lay on my bed with tears springing thickly from my eyes as I recalled his dreamy, frightened looks when he whispered his last words to me.

*   *   *

18

"... I do not know how that madness went up to my head, nor do I know how that whispering warmth slipped into my chest, melting past ice that clung to my heart for many years.

Rebellion sprung from her eyes a challenge and irony, playing a strong melody of life in her body and soul. For the first time I see this charming harmony between the soul and the body, between color and melody, between madness and reason. A bit of madness drives me to a stupor, my soul slipping from me to her, my body not mine, it seemed to melt into her soul, into her warm transparent body. Do not think I didn't know women before her......"

He said, suddenly pulling his eyes from the sea and turning to Selim, who has remained silent, amazement holding his tongue ...

"... No ... no ... my friend, I had known many women before her but they all remained silent playthings, their blood cold and icy as they relaxed into melting gel after the end of the permanent game of the body. Cold gripped my chest after all this, I flinch away then wrap myself in a ball, as I feel that terrible emptiness playing deep down inside me.

Do you know what a facade is? Yes a facade... that glazed glass surface, that noise panting after heavy machinery is what we know there. As for the internal reality, this divergent depth, the sound of Nirvana, the happiness of drinking one's fill, it was what I had missed since my early childhood. I reached out for it with my eyes but I did not touch it, I touched it with my eyelashes but I kept afloat on the surface, defeated by the sky. It seemed to me that my fate is this golden shiny surface, that I will not go beyond this impossible horizon, until Julia came ... "

He fell silent as his gaze went out to the sea; he put his head between his shoulders and drowned in a hazy dream.

Selim was looking at him confusedly, contemplating his forehead, which had become wrinkled. It seemed to him that he must do something, yet when he reached to touch his hand compassionately, he quickly retreated as he saw Roger's eyes close and his lean hands began strongly pulling on his face. Selim's eyes fled to the sea, adrift on an ocean of sadness as both men became lost in distant memories..

*

... The fog was slowly dispelled by the cool wind gently blowing through the green dewy branches, circling their necks, as they lay on the ground in close proximity. For a while they had been silent, their eyes flying to the sky covered by black clouds. Suddenly the rain started falling lightly.

He mopped off the raindrops, which scattered on his face and then began to rise, saying:

"We have to get in before the rain increases."

"Please don't move. Let us stay as we are."

"But it is raining!"

"Raining! And what business it is of ours? Let it rain as it likes." She retorted, disgruntled, without taking her eyes from the sky. So, he went back to lie down next to her, pressing his face to her face, feeling the warmth of her short, black hair.

"Look at the clouds, after a while, they will fuse together and that gap will disappear."

"Yes, the sky will become fully black, shortly."

"Then the sky will explode and the rain will fall in abundance."

"That is what I was saying."

"We will be drenched with rain soaking our bodies."

"Yes, perhaps we will catch a cold."

She looked at him suddenly, her eyes sparkling with a mixture of anger and defiance:

"Kiss me!"

He stared at her with astonishment and then turns towards her, he touches his lips to hers and embraces her head with his lean hands. He felt her warm breath on his lips as she closed her eyes. He squeezed her lips voraciously but the rain that kept falling profusely made him rise up, shouting:

"Come on, let's take shelter under one of the trees. Our clothes are soaked through."

She remained silent and motionless as she stared at him with defiant, crazy looks. Rain poured profusely over her face and body, her long black dress dropped to her knees and her breasts were hidden behind her thick, woolen pullover.

"Come on Julia, before you are soaking wet."

She stands slowly, without leaving his eyes and says in something of a whisper:

"Why don't we run a little bit?"

"But, Julia ..."

"Come on ... Come on, the rain is beautiful."

She grabbed his hand suddenly and starts jogging. He responds to her impulse and runs near her. They kept running over the green wet ground, meandering around the various fruit trees as they delved into the spacious orchard. The rain had soaked their clothes and leaked to their bodies when she said, laughingly egging him on:

"Quickly, quickly ... oh, how lazy you are!"

He hurried up, trying to keep up with her and he feels the pain in his chest getting worse but he rushed over, beat the earth with his feet and sped up. He felt her challenging eyes, those sarcastic glances touching him sideways, so he pressed even more and ran as hard as he could. It seemed to him that he was engaged in his last race. 'I will not let her defeat me,' he thought as he let go of her hand and ran fast, beating her by a short distance. She screamed at him, laughingly:

"Ha, ha, ha ... ha, ha, ha ... faster ... more ... more ... I will reach you."

He felt her hand touching him, so he gathered the remnants of his energy and ran even faster. 'She will never defeat me!' He pressed his teeth so hard, trying to resist that extreme weight that kept squeezing his chest strongly. Still, her hand suddenly fell on his shoulder as she pulled him back, so he stopped and turned around to her.

"Kiss me!" She demanded through quick successive breaths, as she stared into his eyes.

He stood in front of her for a little while, trying to catch his breath as he put his hand on his heart, which was beating violently but she does not allow him the chance to do so. She throws herself onto him, her hands on his shoulders and touches her lips to his lips. He holds her to him, trying to kiss her but her successive, rapid pants prevent that. He feels his lips droop inadequately, so he pressed them violently on her lips while his eyes flee far away, wrapped in a dense fog. She pushes him gently away as her eyes slip to the ground. She takes a few steps beyond him, towards a nearby tree. She stands there contemplating him, as rain soaked him entirely through, while water dropped from his hair to his face and neck. Her eyes met his eyes and freeze for a moment, then she takes off her pullover, throws it on the ground and she moves towards him, saying:

"I want to dance."

The sky had fallen into turmoil, the sounds of thunder and

flashing of lightning spread deep into it. He stared into her face and then draws a smile on his lips as he feels his chest rest and his breath calm down.

The dream approaches closer and closer, until it fuses to her eyes as she wriggles on the green wet grass. Her eyes are streaming and laughing tremors, the body a wildfire ignition, glowing in the pouring rain and the wind fleeing to its ancient burial ground. He stood dreamingly contemplating her body, floating slowly like a butterfly around a wildflower just opened. Heavy rain washed her face, falling sideways onto her dress, which stuck to her skin exposing her body in harmonious, magnificent detail.

"Why aren't you dancing?" She yelled at him, as she played with her hand swaying in the air. Her body was a brazen call and her eyes were fiery meteors raging noisily, while he was sailing in the flowing waterfall of the folds of her fiery body. She picked up his hand and pulled him toward her.

"Come on, dance like me."

His body twists harshly as he watches her graceful movements, trying to imitate her.

"Open your hands like that ... Yes, yes like that ... Let them move freely."

Warmth slipped into his chest bit by bit, the shards of ice between his ribs fading as he writhed around her, while his eyes melted in the euphoria of warmth, which spilled onto her face and madness slipped to his core until his body languished around her, flying ..., flying without knowing where, while she whirled around her soft legs. He was like a small body, revolving in her nebular orbit. He felt the deprivation of things, the insanity of the outside; the inside is something nihilistic and silent. They are alone, dancing, without melody or song, without a whisper of nature, alone in a vacuum of silence hanging with charm and serenity. The intensity of the falling rain increased and lightening rent the sky, so their bodies are strained and their movements accelerate as they shake violently and harmoniously. Their hearts beat strongly and the sky turned to a berserk volcano, coloring the clouds with a pink intermittent light, while the voices of their gasps are mixed with the breath of wind.

"Kiss me!" She suddenly whispered, stopped and closed her eyes.

He stood in front of her, panting and looking at her with awe.

"Kiss me!" She roared through her small white teeth.

He felt her hot breaths enter his mouth as he swallows her lips. So, he pulled her to him, pressing down her chest to his and drowns in her fading body, like a wave of fog and wind. His soul melted into her soul and the trembling wings fluttered in his chest, consuming him in a coma of intoxication that took him deep into a nihilistic, transparent soft nebula.

*

He suddenly opened his eyes and looked at the street where a sudden bustle emerged, followed by the launch of a burst of bullets. The street was filled with militants who had started to inspect passing cars. He looked up to Selim inquiringly, with his perplexity increasing:

"What's going on?"

"It's the militia of one of the parties; it seems this is a flying barrier ..."

They returned to silence as they observed what was going on with concern. They had often heard about these barriers, which would be erected suddenly and continue for some minutes, then disappear, leaving behind them a number of victims. However, the militants quickly left the place in the same bustle that announced their arrival, after having stopped one of the cars, inspected identity cards but without anything that they were expecting, happening.

"It seems that they are pursuing someone." Selim said as

he turned to Roger, who had regained his composure, whilst he contemplated the faces of other customers who had also resumed their smiles and drowned in the commotion of their excited conversations.

"I feared something terrible would happen." Roger commented, as his eyes pursued the bustle of cars in the street, which had regained its normal flow of traffic.

"Yes, the conditions in Beirut have changed a lot since the massacre in Ain el-Rommaneh.[19]"

"But why this violence?"

"Violence! ... I don't know."

Selim looked at him in bewilderment and then continued with some impatience:

"But why do we not go back to where we were? You did not finish your speech, what happened after that?"

"Ah ... yes, my friend ..." He said confusedly, returning back with his eyes to the sea. He drowned in a short silence and then he said:

"We would meet daily in that huge orchard, hiding among its trees, embracing in a trance of a happy dream. We would stay there until noon and then say goodbye, before the return of her uncle and his two sons.

She was staying in her uncle's house, an Aleppan wheat trader, after she returned from Damascus, where she'd received her high school education, hosted by her uncle, a doctor. After her father died she had lived with him until she was returned to her uncle, the grain dealer. She felt tightness and fear of her new uncle, who had placed her within the walls of his home and forbade her to go out. However, his wife, that good old lady who didn't have any female children with him, was compassionate toward her and allowed her to stroll in the rear garden, on condition that she returned before her uncle came home from his work. She often requested her uncle, the doctor, to take her back to Damascus but he was want to anger his brother, saying:

'I do not want my brother to curse me in his grave.'

She was not yet used to that walled isolation, which separated her from the other life. Her uncle in Damascus was a cultured man who had lived in France for a long time before returning to settle in Damascus, with his French wife.

His wife was barren, thus making them welcome her as an only daughter upon whom they bestowed special affection. So, she lived blessed with that freedom that only a few of her colleagues had at the time. However, when she moved to Aleppo, everything changed. Her uncle insisted on switching her 'Frankish' clothes, as he used to call them, dressing her more modestly. Then entrusted her to his wife, to train her on home life and qualify her to become a, 'good wife.'

I used to feel a beam of rebellion flowing from her eyes when she spoke about her life. She turned into a wolf with harsh looks as she stared at me, saying:

'I will not be what he wants me to be!'

The beam of hope pulled at me so I said impatiently:

'Why don't we leave together?'

'How?'

'Get married and depart to France.'

'But they will never accept it, they hate the French. If they find out about my relationship with you, they would tear both of us to pieces.'

'But what can we do?'

'I don't know ...'

And we would go back to our oblivion, deluged in our ecstasy, dallying with our happy spirits, until she came to me on that fateful day, frightened and scared to tell me that she was pregnant... "

*   *   *

19

10. 5. 1972

Can I etch the memories of that day on my body? Can I take record of that day with my blood? I don't know but just today I found out what it means to be reborn after death, to rejoice after misery. For in spite of his letter, in which he told me he is coming. In spite of his telegraph that determines the date of his arrival as today, I have remained unbelieving. Even when he came towards me down the airport hall, extending his hands in front of him, ready to embrace me, it seemed to me that I was recalling an old dream and that I am still in my bed. Only when his hands crept into my hair, as he caught my head in his hands whispering:

'How I have waited for you Zenobia!' Was I able to realize what the word, 'truth' means.

He could not wait; we stayed throughout that day recalling old memories. He told me about his long prison term, his permanent torment in search of news of me and how he returned to his country, defeated and devastated after the long years of his imprisonment. He told me about the ice that returned to his body, about the bitter cold that clung to his guts, about things departing with him from one bar to another; from one silence to another, as he searched for the warmth of the past and for that quiver of hope pulsing in his chest. I embraced him as in the past; I kissed him with quivering lips searching for an old, insane love. I put my head on his chest as I confided my misery to him, my scattered spirit behind the shores of fear and I realized that we were one misery.

I returned shortly after midnight. I left him deep asleep, after he resisted his exhaustion for a long time. Things were quickly taking color and my body was a mass of soft feathers, flying lightly and quietly above the asphalt of the small street that leads to my apartment. I don't know if I can sleep today, for the dream assaults me with past shivers and anxiety. It is a whip, searing me as I contemplate Selim sleeping next to me.

11. 2. 1972

I have asked for leave that day. The manager could not refuse my request in spite of the signs of annoyance that appeared on his face. But what could I have done? Roger has called me and insisted on seeing me this morning. I have felt the tension that accompanies his voice when he suffers intense fatigue and exhaustion.

He really was tired, to the point of collapse; his eyes red and concerned, pallor encased his face in a mask of death. He asked me to manage a meeting between him and Soha. He surprised me by his request and I could only scream, objecting to that. I repeated the words I said to him earlier:

'She is not your daughter, you are mistaken.'

Yet, he was sure that she was his daughter and wanted to get her back, in spite of everything. My visit did not last a long time; for soon his anger intensified, he accused me of treason and that I am trying to withhold his right to see his daughter. I went out angry, without him being able to force me to admit anything. He thinks he would make her happy, what a misery! Does he not know that he would do nothing but worry her and increase her misery?

1. 15. 1973

The mad man did it. It seemed to me that he would not dare to do so. He managed to get her address. He sent her a letter telling her everything, stressing his desire to meet her quickly. I felt the threads of my will slip out of my hand. So, my screams were raised in anger and reprimand but he was angrier and even more strained than I was. We were sinking into a noisy fight as we exchanged accusations, recalling a far away past, which flew rapidly through our livid words. However, I soon collapsed, after recognizing that I was fighting something impossible to resist. I realized that he knows very well details that I thought had faded into oblivion. Although he was in prison, no one could prevent him from following-up on my news. I have promised to reform everything but I do not know if I am able to fulfill my promise.

* * *

20

"... It was necessary to do something before it was too late, so I went back to raise the idea of marriage. Even though it was a hopeless matter, she agreed to venture it after other means had rendered us helpless.

Only three months remained of my work in Aleppo. Almost two years had passed since my presence there, so it was necessary to hurry. I resorted to a Syrian employee that I had a strong friendship with. He agreed to help me, after he alerted me to the difficulty of what I was requesting. He knew that family well, especially her uncle, who was with her father in the mountains. However, although he enjoyed the respect of the uncle, he could not move him to change his decision to reject me, saying as he gave me frozen, harsh stares:

'No, Abu Salem, tell this French man to return to his country. My brother's blood is not yet dry.'

I realized then that I would not be able to do anything with this man, who is still looking for past revenge. Thus, I was determined to flee with her. There was nothing else for us to do. They would kill her and maybe kill me as well, if they knew of her pregnancy.

The next day I was waiting for her in the usual place but

my waiting was in vain, as it was in the following days. She
suddenly disappeared and I knew nothing. I experienced a lot
of fear; 'Is it possible that they have found out about it? Did
something wrong happen to her? But no, perhaps they have
forbidden her to go out after I dared to ask to marry her; they
probably guessed that I have a relationship with her.'

I tried as hard as I could to find out any news about her
but everyone locked their doors in my face, saying: 'let her be,
she is not for you.' And what could I have done? I asked
around a lot but the only answer that came back to me was a
terrible silence. So, I sat in my office waiting for the unknown
and what unknown could come, except her pleading
entreating eyes ...

.... More than a month had passed since her disappearance,
when I dared approach the house, looking into the windows
but they were closed and stillness surrounded the place.
When I turned away, I suddenly heard the sound of the
opening of a window, directly above me. I turned quickly and
found her waving her hands and smiling but as soon as I
started to call to her, she closed the window and disappeared
into her dark cave.

Something like madness came over me. What can I do? I
am a foreigner and I don't know anyone. Everyone looks at
me with hatred and I can hope for no one's help. It seemed
to me that life had started to become closed again and fog
rolled over places with a thick cover. I realized what
threatened her, soon her condition would come to light and
the swords of honor would pour heavily on her. I had come
to realize what this word meant in your countries, it had
become associated in my consciousness with blood and
horror. Fear crawled in my chest, so I resorted to my French
friends and acquaintances but they looked at me with disdain,
advising me to quickly return to France.

'I would not be such a scoundrel, I love her!' I shouted in
the face of a friend of mine who worked at the embassy,
when he tried to persuade me to abandon her and return to

France. However, he finally agreed to help me to flee with her to France, after realizing that I would not give her up.

I went back to Aleppo quickly, determined to find a way through which I can tell her I had managed my affairs and now we could escape together to France, where we would get married. Within a few days I managed to send her a message through one of the Syrian girls who worked in our offices. I did not have long to wait; two days later, she was standing in front of me, saying:

'Here, I came!'

I looked at her in astonishment as I observed her eyes glitter strangely and that glamorous smile, hesitating on her lips. It seemed to me that I was seeing her for the first time in that modern dress, which was wrapped on her breasts and hips, strongly highlighting that wonderful harmony of her body. She threw herself on my chest and kissed my neck, saying:

'Come on, Roger we have to leave quickly before they discover my disappearance.'

I was scared by the terror I saw in her eyes as she begged me to hurry up as much as I could. So, I started to prepare for our departure immediately but I had to stop at my nearby office, to leave some necessary paperwork of mine. It was almost eleven a.m. when I took my car toward the office. I did not delay, at half past twelve p.m. I was going up the stairs of the small, two-storey building toward my apartment on the second floor. However, I had only risen several steps when I heard a noisy bustle coming from my residence. So, I hastened my pace over the few steps separating me from the door of my apartment, which I found open. As soon as I entered I saw that terrible scene; she was curled up receiving her uncle's blows. He seemed about to kill her with those huge, steely hands. I pushed him away from her, yelling fiercely at him, as blood flowed to my face:

'Let her be, you criminal, you will kill her.'

The push was strong enough to throw him to the ground but he quickly jumped toward me, with his eyes bulging out of their orbs and blood filaments expanding in the whites of his eyes. I retreated away from him as he approached, extending his hands to my neck. I tried to resist but his strong hands held on to my neck without allowing me a chance to escape. I don't know how that heavy bronze statue came into my hands, nor do I know how it fell on his head. What I saw after that was horrible; he was lying in front of me, drowned in a lake of blood that flowed from his broken head. Severe dizziness hit me as I looked at that hot blood, which splattered my face and clothes. I fell helplessly by his side.

I don't know how much time had passed, before I found myself shackled and led, amid a raucous audience shouting insults at me, across the street toward the waiting police car."

Selim was listening with absolute attentiveness to Roger, observing his face losing its color little by little, his eyes cast down upon the crowded the table, which was covered with untouched foods. As Roger began to recite his story in prison, Selim murmured with his lips, wanting to break up the story, for many questions were jammed in his head and he was no longer able to wait patiently for answers. However, the sight of Roger's suddenly bulging eyes and strange noises silenced him. He turned quickly to see what was causing the commotion. A group of gunmen had stormed into the café. They started approaching them quickly, pointing the barrels of their guns around the café.

"Nobody moves!"

One of them shouted violently, as he directed his rifle towards customers who were suddenly alerted to what was going on and started to watch the insurgents with caution. A terrible silence dominated the café, when three of them circled Roger, who stood with astonishment as he felt the barrels of their guns touching his body.

"Come quickly!" .

One of them shouted as he caught his shoulder and pushed him harshly. Roger stumbled over his chair and would have fallen, were it not for their strong arms, which picked him up quickly and pushed him outside.

Selim was watching what was going on, overwhelmed in a daze but he suddenly woke up and started to scream at them, trying to approach them.

"What is going on? ... Where are you taking him?"

However, a powerful blow struck his jaw and made him groggily stumble over the table, which then flipped over his body, along with the dishes on top of it, causing a loud crash. As soon as he tried to stand up again, he received a severe blow from the butt of a gun and fell unconscious on its impact, as a deluge of blood splattered on his head and face.

* * *

21

... 1975

I have done my best, I can no longer continue. If I leave him, he will kill himself. His eyes tell me so. Can I be the cause of a new tragedy? Only today I felt the hideousness of what I am doing, I felt my excessive selfishness, which is driving me to destroy him in search of my happiness. He came today, devastated and destroyed, as I have never seen him before. His pleading eyes hurled towards me with the ferociousness of the wounded, looking for a sanctuary to shelter him. I felt the insanity of his wounds inflame my face when he approached me, drunk with his blood flowing from his lips. I do not know what happened to him this evening, he probably had a fight with someone, or was hit by a car as he crossed the street and perhaps this and perhaps that ... But is not all this because of me?

I may have been the victim of an unjust life; I may have

been infected with the curse of the ancients but Selim will not be my victim. I have made up my mind today. Roger must understand it; he has to leave and go to his other bank. Our journey has ended.

. . . 1975

Since that stormy night, Selim has been unable to believe what is going on. I realize that clearly; he was shocked by that sudden change in my attitude, his skeptical looks, his hesitancy and permanent fear to lose me. I will try my best to remove those doubts, although I am resisting another tendency that is weakening me. However, I will not go back, I will not let this childish innocence echo my fate.

. . . 1975

Oh what a miserable man! In spite of his silent acceptance of my decision, he continued to frequent the places where we used to meet. Today, I met him by accident while I was wandering with Selim on the seashore; he was sitting silently as he watched the road. My eyes met his eyes and then quickly my look broke away, behind the glass that separated us. Reckless winds swept my breasts, drawing me towards him, I almost shouted: 'Roger!' but Selim's powerful hand that embraced my palm was enough to capture my silence, as I jogged beside him fleeing toward the sea.

. . . 1975

I have agreed to marry him today. I knew that he would return to his demand and I had decided that as long as this was his wish, I would not reject him. He almost danced with *joy when I told him that I consent. It seems to me that he still does not believe; since the morning, he kept repeating to me his desire to travel quickly to do so. Maybe we will leave next week; I will not make him wait for long.*

. . . 1975

I feel very tired after this long day. Immediately we got to this beautiful villa we started to unpack our luggage, without being able to enjoy this magnificent garden that surrounds the villa. Although I am staying here for the second time, yet I feel an alien loneliness step on my chest harshly. Perhaps, because I will share with Selim, this bed that reminds me of my last meeting with Roger. I told Selim I wanted the other room but he remained adamant about staying in this room. I couldn't find a reason to convince him to change his mind; especially because it is the most beautiful room really. Roger did not choose it haphazardly, when we stayed here two months ago.

. . . 1975

This was a pretty great day. I spent it in the garden, accompanied by Selim, who started to portray to me the future happiness that we will enjoy, after we have children. I could not stop him from getting carried away; his heart is strongly pulsing in search of the impossible. I will not take that dream away from him; I will allow him to stay engrossed in his delicious coma as long as it makes him happy. I know I will not give him a lot but I still feel the happiness of giving.

. . . 1975

I do not know what happened to me today; ever since the morning I have been feeling Roger's breath infiltrate the gentle breeze coming through the dense trees, which shade our garden and caress my face. His face was wandering around with me, from one place to another, while his worried sad eyes sank into my eyes. I tried my best to expel his image, seeking refuge with Selim, who was telling me his old tales about his mad aunt but Roger's smile stuck to Selim's lips, to the point that I called him Roger. Suddenly he froze as he looked at me, saying:

"What? Roger!"

"Did I say Roger?"

I answered with a smile, attempting to hide my confusion. Then made amends, saying that yesterday I heard this name on the radio and liked it very much at the time ... he laughed with me a little but I'm not sure that he believed this story.

... 1975

I feel crazy, I'm stuck in the middle of these successive images that drive me towards the past. I don't know what to do. Have I committed a double sin? Maybe, though what else could I have done? Oh, how miserable I am; I leave without knowing where to, I have lost the right path. I thought that I am capable of forgetting but no, he is with me, he lives in my blood cells. I resist his sad pleading eyes, his trembling lips as he says: 'Julia ... Julia ... I will always love you ...' But I come back to find myself drowning in his eyes.

... 1975

I had another fit of pain; I felt my guts being almost torn apart. Selim called the doctor, who decided after examining me, the need for some medical tests at a hospital in Beirut. Selim insisted on cutting our vacation short and returning, in spite of my desire to postpone it. It has become a painful misery for him to suffer, seeing me so emaciated. Is this aging? I have often wondered about it but I always ran away towards my young soul, as I used to think. But my appearance is more revealing and stronger than my assertion. I am tired and feel severe exhaustion. I will try to sleep.

. . . 1975
Oh, the horror of these monotonous days! I stay alone all day waiting for his return. I feel myself a mass of redundant rags, scattered by everyone. Even Georgette's visits have become more spaced and shorter, despite her encouraging words as she comforts me, saying:
"It is only a mild malaise. You will soon beat it."
Only Selim remains beside me, in spite of everything. As soon as he comes back from work, he sits with me trying to entertain me with his tales and joys; his only concern is my comfort. Am I the one who is crazy, or is he? I don't know, I only know that something imminent and violent knocks my head, saying that I alone am responsible for what is happening.

. . . 1975
If I were asked how it happened I would not have been able to answer. My mental powers suddenly collapsed this morning. I couldn't be patient any more, I felt myself being led to him, bereft of any self-will. I threw myself on his chest like a crazy teenager and he seemed like he was crucified, his distraught looks hitting a void. I cannot express everything that happened, my thoughts and feelings are crowded and billowy, like waves in a sea covered with heavy froth. All I can say is

that I felt my strength returning to me, my soul regaining its brilliance anew ... I love him ... I love him madly ... I go to sleep between his arms, like a girl caressed by the dream of a near date. But, for how long? Oh, I am miserable! Silence is the only answer of the helpless.

... 1975
I will not go beyond that; my spirit is torn and stolen. I feel my torn limbs scattered under my dress and rain pouring down into internal emptiness ...

My turn has come to pick up my happiness, which had escaped me for a long time ...

* * *

22

He had been a prisoner in his small apartment for weeks; he did not go out of it except in order to provide himself with his needs and then return quickly, before he is hunted by one of the shells that fall suddenly and without warning. He was well aware of what threatened him when he decided to go out in search of food. In spite of the stillness that bathes the street, nobody is tempted by those clear, reassuring skies, for death could suddenly fall; reaping those hungry beings who dared to penetrate the terror barrier, in search of food.

He had just returned from a lightning visit to a nearby shop. He bought a few needs and returned quickly, for in spite of the cease-fire announcement last night, he was well aware that such agreements would only be a trap for more victims.

He looked at the street, crowded with increasingly noisy cars, transporting the piles of human beings fleeing to safer places. He's aware that it's only a temporary truce, after which the streets will become empty, so the madness can begin anew. 'But where can I go?' The question buzzes in his head with a violent rhythm. Many times he had thought about this matter but he was soon back to his uselessness, his head hurting with a severe headache.

For a not inconsiderable time he was no longer linked to Beirut, except by the futile memories of a sad past. It had been more than three months since Rola's disappearance, behind the fiery wall that split Beirut into two parts. He tried to contact her repeatedly by telephone, the lines of which remained, warming the hearts of some people despite the winter cold but the phone merely echoed in her empty house. Even Georgette Nassor, the woman drowning in the hustle and bustle of life, had traveled to France two weeks ago, after informing him that she could no longer do anything about finding Roger, who had disappeared without leaving a trace. He had resorted to her immediately. Yet, as soon as she heard what happened, she went mad and ran out screaming:

"They will kill him; they will kill him if you do not hurry up!"

He was surprised by her odd reaction; he didn't even know she knew him. It seemed to him she was almost about to go mad when he told her what had happened to him. She contacted all her acquaintances to try to save him. She ran from one place to another in search of him but found no trace. She continued to rebel against friends' advice to stop looking for him, roaming Beirut's secret offices, begging sometimes and angry at others. Until one day someone came to tell her that he is still alive but that he will not continue to be if she didn't stop searching for him and leave.

She told Selim that, saying with a bit of sad irony:

"We have to leave my friend, before the rest leave us behind."

Yet he remained, the only one behind the departing train.

His ears picked up sounds of distant shots, mixed with intermittent explosions. His eyes jerked toward the direction the noise came from. He didn't notice any change in the busy street traffic, so he returned to the living room without closing the window.

'Where did this mad man disappear to? Why didn't he tell me that he would be away for a long time?' He thought as he relaxed in his big chair, while his fingers picked up a cigarette from a pack that was on the small table in front of him. 'This damned worm, he hardly ever settles in his place!' He threw the snuffed out matchstick on the small carpet, after nervously lighting the cigarette. He was feeling concern mixed with anger at Reda's long absence, for he was the only one who kept visiting him, sharing the house with him every now and then. He was bound to him by a strong friendship after he met him by chance, at one of the armed checkpoints.

He was returning home from his work, suffering intense fatigue and exhaustion, after being detained by a battle that suddenly broke out in the street where his office was located. He had stayed for hours, glued to the ground with one of the female employees who had clung to his arm, panicked, crying and screaming:

"Please, Mr. Selim, do not leave me alone! Please, they will kill me!"

He was aware that there was nothing he could do for her but he had tried to reassure her as best he could, until the guns had fallen silent and the combatants retreated to their previous positions. He waited to be sure that the street had become safe, then he went across one of the back streets, accompanied by his colleague. Then, they got into a taxi, which took them to her nearby home. He did not accept her invitation to dinner, preferring to return to his apartment quickly, before it got dark.

When the car that was taking him to his apartment stopped, he was still suffering from the effects of those horrific atrocities that he'd escaped only a short while ago. His heart pounded as he watched the barrels of their guns directed toward his chest, while one of them started to check his identity card.

"Selim el-Radi!" The armed young man said, as he looked at him in astonishment.

"Yes, Selim el-Radi, a Syrian. I work in an office close to here and I do not have anything to do with what is going on." Selim responded mechanically, as one used to uttering these answers, which he offered everywhere.

"Don't you remember me, Mr. Selim?"

Selim scrutinized his face. He seemed to him a boy, no more than fifteen, with those black hairs that were scattered on his chin. Except, his tall lean stature along with his military tone, made him appear older than suggested by his face.

"Excuse me; I do not recall that I saw you before. Will you introduce yourself to me?"

"Reda Hamdan."

"Reda Hamdan! ... I am sorry, my friend, it seems that my memory has betrayed me again."

"Yes, I know that. I was still a kid at the time and you were a prisoner ..." Reda said with a smile and then gave him his identity card. He took it saying:

"Are you saying you saw me in prison?"

"Of course, Mr. Selim. You were still a prisoner when my mom sent me to bring you a message from Julia, don't you remember? You were bearded and had a long head of hair. You were sitting alone in that dirty room and I remember that you gave me a small message at the time and told me: 'Upon her mouth. Do not forget; upon her mouth.'"

Reda's lean face seemed to flush with a childish, innocent smile while he was repeating his last words. Selim was listening to his words, without leaving that smile that brought him memories of that day when that little boy came to him, carrying Julia's message, telling him that she would be waiting for him when he was released. He remembered this sly smile as he slipped him a hidden message.

"Reda! Yes, I remember you very well, you are Reda bin Said Hamdan. How you have grown up, Reda, you have become a young man. Ah, how could I forget that day! You had brought me the happiest news of my whole life."

"And you also have changed a lot but for the name I wouldn't have been able to recognize you."

Reda stopped a little to observe his face and then continued abstractedly:

"But you did not tell me; how is Julia?"

"Julia! ..."

He looked at him with absent eyes, then continued in a whisper:

"She died two months ago."

Reda's eyes were almost implanted in Selim's eyes in disbelief, until he saw Selim's broken look fleeing to the street, avoiding his eyes. So, his eyes also turned toward the asphalt as he whispered:

"I'm sorry, I wanted to see her."

"She would have been very happy to see you but fate was much faster."

"Yes, I have come too late."

"Have you been in Beirut for a long while?"

"No, just a month ago."

"But what are you doing here? Did something happen to your mother?"

"Not at all, she is fine but I have become a fedayee[20]."

"A Fedayeen!"

"Yes, I am fighting for the cause."

"What have you got Reda? Is there anything that you suspect?" A bearded young man roared as he moved towards the car, brandishing his heavy black gun.

"No, he's an old friend passing over here by chance."

"We have no time for that, Reda. Come on, we have to go back right away. You can talk to him later."

A group of young armed men circled around the bearded man quickly, as he issued his orders aloud. Reda apologized to Selim after taking his address, promised to visit him at the earliest opportunity, then jogged around to one of the military vehicles that took off quickly, leaving the other cars behind.

Their friendship was firmly established almost at once. Since the first meeting, he realized that this young man, despite his youth, had the ability to win over the hearts of others towards his cause; which he explained the justice of with the wonderful enthusiasm of a man who is ready to do everything for the cause he believes in. He felt he was talking with a man who was toughened by a harsh, steely life. For, although aware of the dangers to which he would be exposed, he was happily waiting for a murdering bullet like someone who would meet his beloved, after a long separation.

He frequently came by wearing his military uniform with the gleaming black gun that never left him, hung from his shoulders. He felt something sacred and captivating, bonding him to this boy whom he'd suddenly fallen upon, mitigating the impact of the dry life spent amid the death and destruction staring at him from all sides. He came to share his house every now and then. On the days when battles raged and his need for a companion to relieve the pain and fear of loneliness, Reda would suddenly show up, with his permanent smile glittering on his lips; without forgetting to bring their desperately required food and cigarettes. He spent some time with him, telling him the results of his battles, his eyes glittering with the sparkle of a dreamer; while repeating his confident words of near victory. Selim would listen to him, looking at his face with surprise tinged with concern, feeling that trembling glare flowing in his chest, delicious and refreshing.

He began to feel very concerned about him; he was not usually absent for long periods. The only time that he remembered he was absent for a long while, it did not exceed four days. He then returned to apologize, saying that he'd had to go for a far away mission and did not have enough time to inform him. Yet, today he has been absent for nearly a week. 'Is he gone for an urgent mission? ... Maybe; what a lot of work he has, he hardly ever sits before he would jump up to pursue an errand that he had forgotten. Yet, what if something has happened to him?!'

The doorbell rang, bailing him out of his thoughts. So, he jumped immediately heading towards the door with a brightened face. Yet, as soon as he opened the door his face returned to his former frown, when he saw it was his old neighbor. She came to tell him she was departing to her remote village and to ask him to take care of her apartment and be alert to thieves, who were no longer inhibited by any impediment.

He closed the door after her and returned to the living room, having assured her that he will be vigilant and will not allow anyone to enter her apartment. He lit a cigarette and started to leaf through a picture magazine that he brought with him that morning. He went through it quickly, without finding anything in it to diffuse his boredom, for it was full of images of dead people and devastated districts. He stopped a little at the last pages, which were assigned to one of the American actresses and then he tossed the magazine out on the small table in front of him. He felt a light ache in his stomach, so he stood up and started to pace the room back and forth.

'Did she travel abroad? ... And why not? I don't think that her father will remain in Beirut in the middle of all this horror. But why didn't she tell me? ... She could have done so if she'd wanted to.' Rola overwhelmed him with her face, brimful of life and her cheeky smiles. So, he could do nothing but repeat to himself those ideas that echoed in his head a thousand times.

Their relationship had returned to normal after a new love had blossomed in his heart, when that crazy war started and the swords of death hung to cleave Beirut into two parts.

He often wondered about the reasons that kept him in Beirut. Her spirit was his only answer. For months he had waited but nothing indicated the near departure of the mighty sword of Damocles hanging over Beirut. His eyes would search every day for a hope to warm his heart but the sounds of the raging battle, hurled his dream down to rock bottom. Yet, he kept waiting. The waiting was a secret that he hid even from Reda and perhaps from himself too, when the desire to leave raged inside him. He often thought to leave

Beirut to go to another place, until he is able to come back after peace returns but he always backed down for fear of the distance defeating him, so he wouldn't come back.

A sense of fear attacked him when he became alerted to the sounds of heavy shots that rose suddenly and were coming closer and closer. He rushed quickly toward the bedroom and peered out the window to discover what was going on. The street was still crowded but the traffic had changed; the last section of the street was now filled with militants. The ordinary cars had turned back in almost the middle of the street, to go into a side street leading to the sea. He didn't have to listen for long to realize that a fierce battle had begun behind those buildings that walled the end of the street. He felt horrified to perceive it would not be long before he found himself surrounded by death.

He smacked his lips, which were covered in an intensely saline layer. He tossed his half smoked cigarette, then left the bedroom to go to the kitchen, where he prepared a cup of tea and returned to the living room.

He sat silently as he listened to the sounds of the raging battle.

'If only he would come back now!' He thought, as he sucked his next cigarette greedily. 'Maybe he would be able to find me a safer place.' His eyes suddenly caught Julia's picture, hanging in front of him; he began to contemplate it as he lost himself in the memories of their first meeting. He felt the warmth seep into his body as his mind wandered around in the orchards of the village, accompanied by Julia holding his arm and plunging into intermittent laughter, which trembled in his ears and fell on his eyes in a delicious dream, as he fell asleep on a pillow near him.

He didn't know how much time had passed while he was asleep, when he was awakened by that terrible explosion, which made him jerk in panic and then roll down onto the ground, in an involuntarily movement. He thought that a rocket had fallen on the building where he lived, so he kept listening to the outside without moving. He felt something strange had occurred in the street, for the sounds of traffic that were buzzing in his ears a little while ago, had disappeared. He straightened up onto his feet and entered the bedroom, cautiously approaching the open window; the street was empty, except for a broken car near a fierce fire in a building where one of the balconies was destroyed. He noted the presence of some militants, who hid behind the corners of nearby buildings as they brandished their rifles toward the battle site, which seemed as if it had moved to this street. Some stray bullets kept buzzing and whistling in the street and then hit the walls of old buildings.

"If only I had a gun, what an idiot! Why did I refuse his offer?" He muttered, reaching out to pick up the teacup, which he had not touched. He felt that cold bitter taste on his lips, so he threw it to the ground to shatter into small pieces, screaming in exasperation:

"I could have kept it as a precautionary measure!"

He froze suddenly, as he heard the outside bell ringing. He felt something heavy clinging to him, so he remained silent as he stared at the door. The bell returned to beat his ears with its ringing, which was mixed with the sounds of shots outside. He lingered momentarily without moving, his eyes not leaving the wooden door. Then, he suddenly jumped toward the door with brightened features. His chest beat heavily when he saw three militants, armed with machine guns hanging from their hands, slanted downwards.

One of them said as he combed his bushy mustache, which covered his mouth:

"Is this Selim el-Radi's house?"

"Yes. I am Selim."

"You are Reda's relative, right?"

"Yes ... yes, do you have news from him?" He said excitedly, as his eyes rushed into their faces, trying to find something to reassure him.

"... Certainly, but will you not allow us to enter?"

"Ah, excuse me, I was surprised by your presence, I am

waiting for him. Come on in, come on in."

They entered the living room and their eyes searched the small room without sitting down.

"Come on in, please sit down."

"No thank you, we do not have the time, please excuse us."

"Is he all right?"

The young man, who seemed to be the only one with the God-given ability to talk, stared at him, while the other two remained silent, their eyes looking down to the floor, sadly. Selim felt the weight of his stare, so he asked appalled, his limbs drooping:

"Did something happen to him?"

"We are sorry, Mr. Selim, he had been a wonderful companion."

"...!?"

"We are sad to convey to you the news of his martyrdom[21]."

He felt a mass of ice landing on his head, pressing on his chest violently. He threw himself on his chair, embracing his face with his hands, without being able to hear the usual words the young man was repeating to him. He felt a dense fog closing in on his eyes and his ears, swirling violently.

"Mr. Selim ... Mr. Selim! ..."

He felt his hand shaking his shoulder as he called to him.

"Excuse us Mr. Selim, but we have to return quickly. We have to transport his body today to his village. It has been two days since his death."

"Two days!" Selim exclaimed, as he stared him in the eyes
                                            with astonishment.

"Yes, Mr. Selim. We have come to you according to his will. He remembered with his last breath, that he promised you his rifle. Here you are, it's yours." The young man said as he offered him that small gun that Reda always held close, even while lying in bed to sleep.

Selim looked at the clean black gun, then took it from the hand of the young man and kissed it gently, embracing its glossy barrel.

"Excuse me, Mr. Selim. We understand what you are going through but we have to alert you to the fact that you are in grave danger if you stay here. Dark will not come before you are in the middle of the battle. They have mobilized large numbers to break into this street and I don't think we'll be able to withstand them for long."

Selim remained silent. It did not seem that he heard what the young man, who seemed gentle and polite in spite of his harsh appearance, was saying.

They lingered a little as they looked at him in silence and then they turned to go but the young man paused in the door a moment, as he said in a loud voice:

"Try to find yourself a safer place."

Selim heard the sound of the door as it banged shut behind them; then he raised his head, listening to the quick shots that rang violently in his ears. He looked at the door with blazing eyes. Suddenly, he jumped up like someone who'd just remembered something.

They had not gone by the first floor when they heard the sound of his shouts as he called to them, while he descended the stairs quickly.

"Hey ... Hey ... Wait, wait a moment."

He stopped several steps away from them and said, panting:

"Can't I return with you?"

They looked at him with a bit of surprise, as they contemplated his face covered with severe pallor, while Reda's rifle dangled from his hand that caught its middle firmly.

"I will not bother you, I will sit near Reda."

They looked into each other's faces for a moment, then the young man said with a smile:

"Come quickly, there is still room in the hearse!"

WAJDY MUSTAFA

Appendix:

1. Om Hazem: Hazem's mother. Calling a woman by her son's name is a form of expressing respect, especially in rural areas.

2. My sister: A form of addressing familiar women, usually used by women not men.

3. Thanaweya Amma: is equivalent to high school exams. In Arab countries, the results of Thanaweya Amma decide the future studies of the student and which faculty they can join.

4. Abo Saeed: Saeed's father. Calling a man by his son's name is a form of expressing respect, especially in rural areas. Abo Saeed and Om Saeed are Abbas and his wife, the family who returned to the village according to Selim's aunt and her neighbor's gossip.

5. 'Salam': means peace.

6. It is quite unacceptable for young men to smoke in the presence of their elders in Arab countries, more so in small towns and rural areas.

7. Kohl: cosmetic powder used in the East to darken the eyelids (similar to eyeliner.)
8. A diplomatic way of criticizing someone for waiting too long to visit someone who has become a close acquaintance, for the first time.

9. Castle prison is in a small town called Safita in Tartus province in Syria.

10. Piaster: The smallest unit of Egyptian currency (used in

the eastern area of the Mediterranean at the time), like a penny.

11.   Qdameh:
(Turkish: leblebi, Arabic: Qdameh or Qudamah)   is
a snack made from roasted chickpeas, common and popular in Algeria, Iran and Turkey. It is sometimes seasoned with salt, hot spices, dried cloves or candy coated. (From Wikipedia.)

12. Hamra Street in Beirut: a street famous for its cafés, nightclubs and bars that attract people of different ages and social classes.

13. In Arabic 'Selim' means faultless, or well and whole. The question "What is wrong with you?" is a sarcastic reference to the second meaning. The fact that he took another man's wife is a pun on the first meaning.

14. Sordid is the name of your mother you atheist: The worst possible insult an Arab would direct at another is badmouthing the insulted party's mother. To add the adjective, "atheist" to the insult, is like condemning the insulted party to ever after hell as well as insulting them in this life. Arabs, (whether Muslims or Christians) have an unshakable belief that atheists are going straight to hell, for eternity.
15. Mr. Jameel: This would be his first name. Arabs rarely use family names except in very formal, or official circumstances.

16. It is very inhospitable to let a guest leave without walking him/her to the door. In the Arab world, that is akin to throwing the guest out of your home.

17. Home: Our home country.

18. 40th day memory: This is a traditional memorial of the dead, the family gathers and certain ceremonies/rituals are performed in memory of the departed on the 40th day after his/her death. The 40th Day has a major significance in traditions of the orient. It is believed that the soul of the departed remains wandering the Earth during the 40 day period, coming back home, visiting places the departed has lived in as well as his fresh grave. The rituals of that day aim at letting the soul go, in order to keep it from returning and bothering the living. The family visits the grave and then returns to the house of the departed to pray, so the soul of the departed would have peace in its journey to the hereafter.

19. The massacre in Ain el-Rammaneh: Known as The Bus Massacre or 'Ain el-Rammaneh incident' (or 'massacre'.) It was a short series of armed clashes involving Christian Lebanese and Palestinian elements in the streets of central Beirut, which is commonly presented as the spark that set off the Lebanese Civil War in April of 1975.

20. A Fedayeen: one who risks his life in armed struggles, voluntarily sacrificing himself for his country.

21. Martyrdom: Muslims believe that if a fighter dies for the sake of his cause, he becomes a martyr and goes directly to Janna (Heaven).

Also by Wajdy Mustafa

LEVANT FEVER

TRUE STORIES FROM SYRIA'S UNDERGROUND

LEVANT FEVER is a memoir from the political underground darkness of Assad's Syria. Seen through the eyes of a boy growing into a man, in the middle of feverish historic events. Not widely understood, or told before in the West but at the roots of the current conflicts. The narrative grips the reader with its honesty, brutality and beauty. The author describes his own journey, reflections and life stories told to him whilst he was held without trial for 14 years, as a political prisoner in several prisons.